MORIARTY PARADIGM

BASED UPON THE STORIES AND CHARACTERS CREATED BY

SIR ARTHUR CONAN DOYLE

THE SCOUNDREL OF BOHEMIA

BY ADRIAN MIDDLETON

INCORPORATING THE ORIGINAL TEXT OF SIR ARTHUR CONAN DOYLE

Fringeworks

For
David, Damon and Mike
first unto the breech

This edition published in Great Britain in 2014 by
FRINGEWORKS LTD
ISBN: 978-1-909573-19-2

Cover Original cover design: Martin Reimann
Cover Art: Darrel Bevan, with colourisation by Anna Higgins
Cover Format: David R Shires/TheImageDesign

CONTENTS

FOREWORD

As a publisher, it seems somehow wrong to write an entire book yourself but, in the two years of development, the Moriarty Paradigm has become something of a passion for me. From presentations to University conferences to being branded "nothing more than a Doyle plagiarist", it behoves me to get this right, and to take full responsibility by being first on the fence.

Sherlock Holmes has been reimagined more than any other contemporary protagonist, and has already entered into the realms of steampunk, having emerged from the stand alone short stories of the strand into pulp serials, the original fan fiction, pseudo-scholarly studies and a good number of forays into straight and cross-genre continuations, many of which strayed so far from the original that even the most devoted fans wince at his misrepresentation.

This volume contains an unashamed mash-up of the first Holmes story, A Scandal in Bohemia, an original short story introducing our version of Professor James Moriarty, and some supporting articles which I hope will help us capture the feel of the Sherlockiana from days gone by. As the series progresses we will be telling stories that challenge the boundaries of the traditional, touching on pulp adventure, science fiction and horror, but all set within the confines of a believable alternative British Empire shaped by the manipulations of the great detective's greatest enemy.

Which brings us to Moriarty himself, another character reimagined in a hundred different stories. Through the lens of Doyle's fiction, Moriarty appears in only one story, is directly involved in a second, and gets a passing reference in five more. His most significant appearance—where he is named not as James but as Robert Moriarty—is in a lost Holmes play rewritten by the actor William Gillette that gives perhaps the best insight into his character. Our professor is very much at the heart of Holmes' world, appearing indirectly in many of the tales that we intend to tell, his own story unfolding as the years roll by.

It's an adventure we're looking forward to.

ADRIAN MIDDLETON, 2014
Birmingham, West Midlands

I. The Man in the Vizard Mask

To Sherlock Holmes she is always the woman. I have seldom heard him mention her under any other name. In his eyes she eclipses and predominates the whole of her sex. It was not that he felt any emotion akin to love for Irene Adler. He represented all emotions, and that one particularly, as abhorrent to his cold, precise but admirably balanced mind. He was, I take it, the most perfect reasoning and observing machine that the world has seen, but as a lover he would have placed himself in a false position. He never spoke of the softer passions, save with a gibe and a sneer. They were admirable things for the observer—excellent for drawing the veil from men's motives and actions. But for the trained reasoner to admit such intrusions into his own delicate and finely adjusted temperament was to introduce a distracting factor which might throw a doubt upon all his mental results. Grit in a sensitive instrument, or a crack in one of his own high-power lenses, would not be more disturbing than a strong emotion in a nature such as his. And yet there was but one woman to him, and that woman was the late Irene Adler, of dubious and questionable memory.

I had seen little of Holmes lately. Matters between us were a little tender after I had been declared unfit to travel and excluded from his lunar excursion when I received an offer from our mutual friend, Stamford. The opportunity to become a partner in a new civil practice had been too irresistible to turn down, and the move to Farringdon and my sudden and most unexpected marriage to his sister had quickly drifted us away from each other. The new Mrs Watson's previous experience of Holmes had left her critical of both his methods and his demeanour, and her affection towards me was conditional on some distance being put between us. This had been much easier than expected at the time, for I felt unable to explain away the reason for my absence. Besides, my own complete happiness, and the home-centred interests which rise up around the man who first finds himself master of his own establishment, were sufficient to absorb all my attention. Meanwhile Holmes, who loathed every form of society with his whole Bohemian soul, remained in our lodgings in

Baker Street, buried among his old books, and alternating from week to week between cocaine and ambition, the drowsiness of abstinence from the drug, and the fierce energy of his own keen nature. He was still, as ever, deeply attracted by the study of crime, and occupied his immense faculties and extraordinary powers of observation in following out those clues, and clearing up those mysteries which had been abandoned as hopeless by the official police. From time to time I heard some vague account of his doings: of his summons to Odessa in the case of the Trepoff murder, of his clearing up of the singular tragedy of the Atkinson brothers at Trincomalee, and finally of the mission which he had accomplished so delicately and successfully for the reigning family of Holland. Beyond these signs of his activity, however, which I merely shared with all the readers of the daily press, I knew little of my former friend and companion.

***

One night—it was on the twentieth of March, 1888—I was returning from a journey to a patient, when my way led me through Baker Street. As I passed the well-remembered door, which must always be associated in my mind with my wooing, and with the dark incidents of involving the People of the Clouds, I was seized with a keen desire to see Holmes again, and to know how he was employing his extraordinary powers. His rooms were brilliantly lit, and, even as I looked up, I saw his tall, spare figure pass twice in a dark silhouette against the blind. He was pacing the room swiftly, eagerly, with his head sunk upon his chest and his hands clasped behind him. To me, who knew his every mood and habit, his attitude and manner told their own story. He was at work again. He had risen out of his drug-created dreams and was hot upon the scent of some new problem. I rang the bell and was greeted by the page boy, Billy, who led me upstairs to the chamber which had formerly been in part my own. I briefly enquired as to my friend's mood, and he just shrugged. Tipping the boy, I stepped inside to see the apartment was barely changed but for the bright electric lights that changed the room's demeanour and banished the flickering shadows to which I had been accustomed.

He looked as lean and alert as ever. There was little trace of his recent lunar exertions other than a darker shade of hair than I was used to. His manner was not effusive. It seldom was; but he was glad, I think, to see me. With hardly a word spoken, but with a kindly eye, he waved me to an armchair, threw across his case of cigars, and indicated a spirit case and a gasogene in the corner. Then he stood before the fire and looked me over in his singular introspective fashion.

"Wedlock suits you," he remarked. "I think, Watson, that you have put on seven and a half pounds since I saw you."

"Seven!" I answered.

"Indeed, I should have thought a little more. Just a trifle more, I fancy, Watson. And in practice again, I observe. You did not tell me that you intended to go into harness."

"Then, how do you know?"

"I see it, I deduce it. How do I know that you have been getting yourself very wet lately, and that you have a most clumsy and careless servant girl?"

"My dear Holmes," said I, "this is too much. You would certainly have been burned, had you lived a few centuries ago. It is true that I had a country walk on Thursday and came home in a dreadful mess, but as I have changed my clothes I can't imagine how you deduce it. As to Mary Jane, she is incorrigible, and my wife has given her notice, but there, again, I fail to see how you work it out."

He chuckled to himself and rubbed his long, nervous hands together.

"It is simplicity itself," said he; "my eyes tell me that on the inside of your left shoe, just where the firelight strikes it, the leather is scored by six almost parallel cuts. Obviously they have been caused by someone who has very carelessly scraped round the edges of the sole in order to remove crusted mud from it. Hence, you see, my double deduction that you had been out in vile weather, and that you had a particularly malignant boot-slitting specimen of the London slavey. As to your practice, if a gentleman walks into my rooms smelling of iodoform, with a black mark of nitrate of silver upon his right forefinger, and a bulge on the right side of his top-hat to show where he has secreted his stethoscope, I must be dull, indeed, if I do not pronounce him to be an active member of the medical profession."

I could not help laughing at the ease with which he explained his process of deduction. "When I hear you give your reasons," I remarked, "the thing always appears to me to be so ridiculously simple that I could easily do it myself, though at each successive instance of your reasoning I am baffled until you explain your process. And yet I believe that my eyes are as good as yours."

"Quite so," he answered, lighting a cigarette, and throwing himself down into an armchair. "You see, but you do not observe. The distinction is clear. For example, you have frequently seen the steps which lead up from the hall to this room."

"Frequently."

"How often?"

"Well, some hundreds of times."

"Then how many are there?"

"How many? I don't know."

"Quite so! You have not observed. And yet you have seen. That is just my point. Now, I know that there are seventeen steps, because I have both seen and observed. By the way, since you are interested in these little problems, and since you are good enough to chronicle one or two of my trifling experiences, you may be interested in this." He threw over a sheet of thick, pink-tinted notepaper which had been lying open upon the table. "It came by the last post," said he. "Read it aloud."

The note was undated, and without either signature or address.

"There will call upon you to-night, at a quarter to eight o'clock," it said, "a gentleman who desires to consult you upon a matter of the very deepest moment. Your recent services to one of the royal houses of Europe have shown that you are one who may safely be trusted with matters which are of an importance which can hardly be exaggerated. This account of you we have from all quarters received. Be in your chamber then at that hour, and do not take it amiss if your visitor wear a mask."

"This is indeed a mystery," I remarked. "What do you imagine that it means?"

"I have no data yet. It is a capital mistake to theorise before one has data. Insensibly one begins to twist facts to suit theories, instead of theories to suit facts. But the note itself. What do you deduce from it?"

I carefully examined the writing, and the paper upon which it was written.

"The man who wrote it was presumably well to do," I remarked, endeavouring to imitate my companion's processes. "Such paper could not be bought under half a crown a packet. It is peculiarly strong and stiff."

"Peculiar—that is the very word," said Holmes. "It is not an English paper at all. Hold it up to the light."

I did so, and saw a large 'E' with a small 'g,' a 'P,' and a large 'G' with a small 't' woven into the texture of the paper.

"What do you make of that?" asked Holmes.

"The name of the maker, no doubt; or his monogram, rather."

"Not at all. The 'G' with the small 't' stands for 'Gesellschaft,' which is the German for 'Company.' It is a customary contraction like our 'Co.'

'P,' of course, stands for 'Papier.' Now for the 'Eg.' Let us glance at our Continental Gazetteer." He took down a heavy brown volume from his shelves. "Eglow, Eglonitz—here we are, Egria. It is in a German-speaking country—in Bohemia, not far from Karlsbad. 'Remarkable as being the scene of the assassination of Wallenstein, and for its silver mines, numerous glass-factories and its paper-mills.' Ha, ha, my boy, what do you make of that?" His eyes sparkled, and he sent up a great blue triumphant cloud from his cigarette.

"The paper was made in Bohemia," I said.

"Precisely. And the man who wrote the note is a German. Do you note the peculiar construction of the sentence—'This account of you we have from all quarters received.' A Frenchman or Russian could not have written that. It is the German who is so uncourteous to his verbs. It only remains, therefore, to discover what is wanted by this German who writes upon Bohemian paper and prefers wearing a mask to showing his face. And here he comes, if I am not mistaken, to resolve all our doubts."

As he spoke there was the chugging, sound of a gas-motor and the grinding of iron treads against the curb. This was followed shortly after by a sharp pull at the bell.

Holmes whistled.

"A Mannheim-Benz, by the sound," said he. "Yes," he continued, glancing out of the window. "A four seater with a pair of the new Otto engines. Three thousand marks apiece and the devil to bring through the Channel Tunnel. There's money in this case, Watson, if there is nothing else."

"I think that I had better go, Holmes."

"Not a bit, Doctor. Stay where you are. I am lost without my Boswell. And this promises to be interesting. It would be a pity to miss it."

"But your client—"

"Never mind him. I may want your help, and so may he. Here he comes. Sit down in that armchair, Doctor, and give us your best attention."

A slow and heavy step, which had been heard upon the stairs and in the passage, paused immediately outside the door. Then there was a loud and authoritative tap.

"Come in!" said Holmes.

***

A man entered who could hardly have been less than six feet six inches in height, with the chest and limbs of a Hercules. His dress was rich with a richness which would, in England, be looked upon as akin to bad taste. Heavy bands of Astrakhan were slashed across the sleeves and fronts of his double-breasted coat, while the deep blue cloak which was thrown over his shoulders was lined with flame-coloured silk and secured at the neck with a brooch which consisted of a single flaming beryl. Boots which extended halfway up his calves, and which were trimmed at the tops with rich brown fur, completed the impression of barbaric opulence which was suggested by his whole appearance. He carried a broad-brimmed hat in his hand, while he wore across the entirety of his face, extending down over the chin, a black vizard mask, which he had apparently adjusted that very moment, for his hand was still raised to it as he entered. It was an intricately detailed façade made of fine velvet. Not something even the richest of clients would have used for a singular occasion.

"You had my note?" he asked with a deep harsh voice and a strongly marked German accent that exposed the arrogance that his mask had concealed. "I told you that I would call." He looked from one to the other of us, as if uncertain which to address.

"Pray take a seat," said Holmes. "This is my friend and colleague, Dr. Watson, who is occasionally good enough to help me in my cases. Whom have I the honour to address?"

"You may address me as the Count Von Kramm, a Bohemian nobleman. I understand that this gentleman, your friend, is a man of honour and discretion, whom I may trust with a matter of the most extreme importance. If not, I should much prefer to communicate with you alone."

I bridled a little at the idea of being excluded from the consult, but rose to go all the same. Holmes caught me by the wrist and pushed me back into my chair. "It is both, or none," said he, which, given our distance in recent months, quite flattered me. "You may say before this gentleman anything which you may say to me."

The Count shrugged his broad shoulders. "Then I must begin," said he, "by binding you both to absolute secrecy for two years; at the end of that time the matter will be of no importance. At present it is not too much to say that it is of such weight it may have an influence upon European history."

"I promise," said Holmes.

"And I."

"You will excuse this mask," continued our strange visitor. "The august person who employs me wishes his agent to be unknown to you, and I may confess at once that the title by which I have just called myself is not exactly my own."

"I was aware of it," said Holmes dryly.

"The circumstances are of great delicacy, and every precaution has to be taken to quench what might grow to be an immense scandal and seriously compromise one of the reigning families of Europe. To speak plainly, the matter implicates the great House of Ormstein, hereditary kings of Bohemia."

"I was also aware of that," murmured Holmes, settling himself down in his armchair and closing his eyes.

Our visitor glanced with what I took to be surprise at the languid, lounging figure of the man who had been no doubt depicted to him as the most incisive reasoner and most energetic agent in Europe. Holmes slowly reopened his eyes and looked impatiently at his gigantic client.

"If your Majesty would condescend to state your case," he remarked, "I should be better able to advise you."

The man sprang from his chair and paced up and down the room in uncontrollable agitation. Then, with a gesture of desperation, he tore the mask from his face and hurled it upon the ground. It was a face of strong character, with dark, piercing eyes, a broad, but distinguished nose, a thick, hanging lip, and a long, straight chin that suggested a very obstinate resolve.

"You are right," he cried; "I am the King. Why should I attempt to conceal it?"

"Why, indeed?" murmured Holmes. "Your Majesty had not spoken before I was aware that I was addressing Wilhelm Gottsreich Sigismond von Ormstein, Grand Duke of Cassel-Felstein, and hereditary King of Bohemia."

"But you can understand," said our strange visitor, sitting down once more and passing his hand over his high white forehead, "you can understand that I am not accustomed to doing such business in my own person. Yet the matter was so delicate that I could not confide it to an agent without putting myself in his power. I have come incognito from Prague for the purpose of consulting you."

"Then, pray consult," said Holmes, shutting his eyes once more.

"The facts are briefly these: Some five years ago, during a lengthy visit to Warsaw, I made the acquaintance of the well-known adventuress, Irene Adler. The name is no doubt familiar to you."

"Kindly look her up in my index, Doctor," murmured Holmes without opening his eyes. For many years he had adopted a system of docketing all paragraphs concerning men and things, so that it was difficult to name a subject or a person on which he could not at once furnish information. In this case I found her biography sandwiched in between that of a Hebrew rabbi and that of a staff-commander who had written a monograph upon the deep-sea fishes.

"Let me see!" said Holmes. "Hum! Born in New Jersey in the year 1858. Contralto—hum! La Scala, hum! Prima donna Imperial Opera of Warsaw—yes! Retired from operatic stage—ha! Living in London—quite so! Your Majesty, as I understand, became entangled with this young person, wrote her some compromising letters, and is now desirous of getting those letters back."

"Precisely so. But how—"

"Was there a secret marriage?"

"None."

"No legal papers or certificates?"

There was a brief pause.

"None."

"Then I fail to follow your Majesty. If this young person should produce her letters for blackmailing or other purposes, how is she to prove their authenticity?"

"There is the writing."

"Pooh, pooh! Forgery."

"My private note-paper."

"Stolen."

"My own seal."

"Imitated."

"My photograph."

"Bought."

"We were," he paused, "both in the photograph."

"Oh, dear! That is very bad! Your Majesty has indeed committed an indiscretion."

"I was mad—insane."

"You have compromised yourself seriously."

"I was only Crown Prince then. I was young. I am but thirty now."

"It must be recovered."

"We have tried and failed."

"Your Majesty must pay. It must be bought."

"She will not sell."

"Stolen, then."

"Five attempts have been made. Twice burglars in my pay ransacked her house. Once we diverted her luggage when she travelled. Twice she has been waylaid. There has been no result."

"No sign of it?"

"Absolutely none."

Holmes laughed. "It is quite a pretty little problem," said he.

"But a very serious one to me," returned the King reproachfully.

"Very, indeed. And what does she propose to do with the photograph?"

"To ruin me."

"But how?"

"I am about to be married."

"So I have heard."

"To Clotilde Lothman von Saxe-Meningen, second daughter of the King of Scandinavia. You may know

the strict principles of her family. She is herself the very soul of delicacy. A shadow of a doubt as to my conduct would bring the matter to an end."

"And Irene Adler?"

"Threatens to send them the photograph. And she will do it. I know that she will do it. You do not know her, but she has a soul of steel. She has the face of the most beautiful of women, and the mind of the most resolute of men. Rather than I should marry another woman, there are no lengths to which she would not go—none."

"You are sure that she has not sent it yet?"

"I am sure."

"And why?"

"Because she has said that she would send it on the day when the betrothal was publicly proclaimed. That will be next Monday."

"Oh, then we have three days yet," said Holmes with a yawn. "That is very fortunate, as I have one or two matters of importance to look into just at present. Your Majesty will, of course, stay in London for the present?"

"Certainly. You will find me at the Langham under the name of the Count Von Kramm."

"Then I shall drop you a line to let you know how we progress."

"Pray do so. I shall be all anxiety."

"Then, as to money?"

"You have carte blanche."

"Absolutely?"

"I tell you that I would give one of the provinces of my kingdom to have that photograph."

"And for present expenses?"

The King took a heavy chamois leather bag from under his cloak and laid it on the table.

"There are three hundred pounds in gold and seven hundred in notes," he said.

Holmes scribbled a receipt upon a sheet of his note-book and handed it to him.

"And Mademoiselle's address?" he asked.

"Is Briony Lodge, Serpentine Avenue, St. John's Wood."

Holmes took a note of it. "One other question," said he. "Was the photograph a carte de visite or a cabinet?"

"It was a cabinet card."

"Then, goodnight, your Majesty," said he, retrieving the the vizard mask from where the King had thrown it to the floor. Holmes examined it briefly before returning it to his client, "and I trust that we shall soon have some good news for you."

Ushering the King from his rooms, Holmes led him downstairs, pausing in the doorway as if to admire the motorized carriage as the masked nobleman climbed aboard.

"Not the most discrete way to carry

out secret business, eh, Watson," said he as the engine sputtered into life and the Mannheim rolled down the street. "I trust there is more to this affair than meets the eye. Did you notice how his majesty paused when I mentioned legal documents."

"I knew it. He was lying?"

"I think he may have omitted some salient points. I do not particularly like the man, for he is a scoundrel whose opinion of women is so low that he cannot bear to give in to their demands, and cannot stand to be rejected. I suspect there is something else to which Miss Adler may be privy, and a compromising photograph provides all the evidence that she needs to back up her threat. I must think on it, for the case intrigues me."

"Goodnight, Watson," he added abruptly, ushering me outside as a vacant hansom pulled over in response to a wave of his hand. "If you will be good enough to call tomorrow afternoon at three o'clock I should like to chat this little matter over with you."

II. The Briony Lodge

At three o'clock precisely I was at Baker Street, but Holmes had not yet returned. The landlady informed me that he had left the house shortly after eight o'clock in the morning. I sat down beside the fire, however, with the intention of awaiting him, however long he might be. I was already deeply interested in his inquiry, for, though it was surrounded by none of the grim and strange features which were associated with the two crimes which I have already recorded, still, the nature of the case and the exalted station of his client gave it a character of its own. Indeed, apart from the nature of the investigation which my friend had on hand, there was something in his masterly grasp of a situation, and his keen, incisive reasoning, which made it a pleasure to me to study his system of work, and to follow the quick, subtle methods by which he disentangled the most inextricable mysteries. So accustomed was I to his invariable success that the very possibility of his failing had ceased to enter into my head.

It was close upon four before the door opened, and a drunken-looking groom, ill-kempt and side-whiskered, with an inflamed face and disreputable clothes, walked into the room. Accustomed as I was to my friend's amazing powers in the use of disguises, I had to look three times before I was certain that it was indeed he. With a nod he vanished into the bedroom, whence he emerged in five minutes tweed-suited and respectable, as of old. Putting his hands into his pockets, he stretched out his legs in front of the fire and laughed heartily for some minutes.

"Well, really!" he cried, and then he choked and laughed again until he was obliged to lie back, limp and helpless, in the chair.

"What is it?"

"It's quite too funny. I am sure you could never guess how I employed my morning, or what I ended by doing."

"I can't imagine. I suppose that you have been watching the habits, and perhaps the house, of Miss Irene Adler."

"Quite so; but the sequel was rather unusual. I will tell you, however. I left the house a little after eight o'clock this morning in the character of a groom out of work. There is a wonderful sympathy and freemasonry among horsey men. Be

one of them, and you will know all that there is to know. I soon found Briony Lodge. It is a bijou villa, with a garden at the back, but built out in front right up to the road, two stories. Chubb lock to the door. Large sitting-room on the right side, well furnished, with long windows almost to the floor, and those preposterous English window fasteners which a child could open. Behind there was nothing remarkable, save that the passage window could be reached from the top of the coach-house. I walked round it and examined it closely from every point of view, but without noting anything else of interest.

"I then lounged down the street and found, as I expected, that there was a mews in a lane which runs down by one wall of the garden. I lent the ostlers a hand in rubbing down their horses, and received in exchange twopence, a glass of half-and-half, two fills of shag tobacco, and as much information as I could desire about Miss Adler, to say nothing of half a dozen other people in the neighbourhood in whom I was not in the least interested, but whose biographies I was compelled to listen to."

"And what of Irene Adler?" I asked.

"Oh, she has turned all the men's heads down in that part. She is the daintiest thing under a bonnet on this planet. So say the Serpentine-mews, to a man. She lives quietly, sings at concerts, drives out at five every day, and returns at seven sharp for dinner. Seldom goes out at other times, except when she sings. Has only one male visitor, but a good deal of him. He is dark, handsome, and dashing, never calls less than once a day, and often twice. He is a Mr. Godfrey Norton, of the Inner Temple. See the advantages of a cabman as a confidant. They had driven him home a dozen times from Serpentine-mews, and knew all about him. When I had listened to all they had to tell, I began to walk up and down near Briony Lodge once more, and to think over my plan of campaign.

"This Godfrey Norton was evidently an important factor in the matter. He was a lawyer. That sounded ominous. What was the relation between them, and what the object of his repeated visits? Was she his client, his friend, or his mistress? If the former, she had probably transferred the photograph to his keeping? If the latter, it was less likely. On the issue of this question depended whether I should continue my work at Briony Lodge, or turn my attention to the gentleman's chambers in the Temple. It was a delicate point, and it widened the field of my inquiry. I fear that I bore you with these details, but I have to let you see my little difficulties, if you are to understand the situation."

"I am following you closely," I answered.

"I was still balancing the matter in my mind when a hansom cab drove up to Briony Lodge, and a gentleman sprang out. He was a remarkably handsome man, dark, aquiline, and moustached—evidently the man of whom I had heard. He appeared to be in a great hurry, shouted to the cabman to wait, and brushed past the maid who opened the door with the air of a man who was thoroughly at home.

"He was in the house about half an hour, and I could catch glimpses of him in the windows of the sitting-room, pacing up and down, talking excitedly, and waving his arms. Of her I could see nothing. Presently he emerged, looking even more flurried than before. As he stepped up to the cab, he pulled a gold watch from his pocket and looked at it earnestly, 'Drive like the devil,' he shouted, 'first to Gross & Hankey's in Regent Street, and then to the Church of St. Monica in the Edgeware Road. Half a guinea if you do it in twenty minutes!'

"Away they went, and I was just wondering whether I should not do well to follow them when up the lane came a neat little landau, the coachman with his coat only half-buttoned, and his tie under his ear, while all the tags of his harness were sticking out of the buckles. It hadn't pulled up before she shot out of the hall door and into it. I only caught a glimpse of her at the moment, but she was a lovely woman, with a face that a man might die for.

" 'The Church of St. Monica, John,' she cried, 'and half a sovereign if you reach it in twenty minutes.'

"This was quite too good to lose, Watson. I was just balancing whether I should run for it, or whether I should perch behind her landau when a cab came through the street. The driver looked twice at such a shabby fare, but I jumped in before he could object. 'The Church of St. Monica,' said I, 'and half a sovereign if you reach it in twenty minutes.' It was twenty-five minutes to twelve, and of course it was clear enough what was in the wind.

"My cabby drove fast. I don't think I ever drove faster, but the others were there before us. The cab and the landau with their steaming horses were in front of the door when I arrived. I paid the man and hurried into the church. There was not a soul there save the two whom I had followed and a surpliced clergyman, who seemed to be expostulating with them. They were all three standing in a knot in front of the altar. I lounged

up the side aisle like any other idler who has dropped into a church. Suddenly, to my surprise, the three at the altar faced round to me, and Godfrey Norton came running as hard as he could towards me.

" 'Thank God,' he cried. 'You'll do. Come! Come!' "

" 'What then?' I asked.

" 'Come, man, come, only three minutes, or it won't be legal.' "

"I was half-dragged up to the altar, and before I knew where I was I found myself mumbling responses which were whispered in my ear, and vouching for things of which I knew nothing, and generally assisting in the secure tying up of Irene Adler, spinster, to Godfrey Norton, bachelor. It was all done in an instant, and there was the gentleman thanking me on the one side and the lady on the other, while the clergyman beamed on me in front. It was the most preposterous position in which I ever found myself in my life, and it was the thought of it that started me laughing just now. It seems that there had been some informality about their license, that the clergyman absolutely refused to marry them without a witness of some sort, and that my lucky appearance saved the bridegroom from having to sally out into the streets in search of a best man. The bride gave me a sovereign, and I mean to wear it on my watch chain in memory of the occasion."

"This is a very unexpected turn of affairs," said I; "and what then?"

"Well, I found my plans very seriously menaced. It looked as if the pair might take an immediate departure, and so necessitate very prompt and energetic measures on my part. At the church door, however, they separated, he driving back to the Temple, and she to her own house. 'I shall drive out in the park at five as usual,' she said as she left him. I heard no more. They drove away in different directions, and I went off to make my own arrangements."

"Which are?"

"Some cold beef and a glass of beer," he answered, ringing the bell. "I have been too busy to think of food, and I am likely to be busier still this evening. By the way, Doctor, I shall want your co-operation."

"I shall be delighted," said I, as any hint of coolness towards my companion had finally evaporated. It was good to be drawn once more into Holmes' adventures.

"You don't mind breaking the law?"

"Not in the least."

"Nor running a chance of arrest?"

"Not in a good cause."

"Oh, the cause is excellent!"

"Then I am your man."

"I was sure that I might rely on you."

"But what is it you wish?"

"When Mrs. Turner has brought in the tray I will make it clear to you. Now," he said as he turned hungrily on the simple fare that our landlady had provided, "I must discuss it while I eat, for I have not much time. It is nearly five now. In two hours we must be on the scene of action. Miss Irene, or Madame, rather, returns from her drive at seven. We must be at Briony Lodge to meet her."

"And what then?"

"You must leave that to me. I have already arranged what is to occur. There is only one point on which I must insist. You must not interfere, come what may. You understand?"

"I am to be neutral?"

"To do nothing whatever. There will probably be some small unpleasantness. Do not join in it. It will end in my being conveyed into the house. Four or five minutes afterwards the sitting-room window will open. You are to station yourself close to that open window."

"Yes."

"You are to watch me, for I will be visible to you."

"Yes."

"And when I raise my hand—so—you will throw into the room what I give you to throw, and will, at the same time, raise the cry of fire. You quite follow me?"

"Entirely."

"It is nothing very formidable," he said, taking a long cigar-shaped roll from his pocket. "It is an ordinary plumber's smoke-rocket, fitted with a cap at either end to make it self-lighting. Your task is confined to that. When you raise your cry of fire, it will be taken up by quite a number of people. You may then walk to the end of the street, and I will rejoin you in ten minutes. I hope that I have made myself clear?"

"I am to remain neutral, to get near the window, to watch you, and at the signal to throw in this object, then to raise the cry of fire, and to wait you at the corner of the street."

"Precisely."

"Then you may entirely rely on me."

"That is excellent. I think, perhaps, it is almost time that I prepare for the new role I have to play."

***

He disappeared into his bedroom and returned in a few minutes in the character of an amiable and simple-minded Nonconformist clergyman. His broad black hat, his baggy trousers, his white tie, his sympathetic smile, and general look of peering and benevolent curiosity were such as Mr. John Hare alone could have equalled. It was not merely that Holmes changed his costume. His expression, his manner, his very soul seemed to vary with every fresh part that he assumed. The stage lost a fine actor, even as science lost an acute reasoner, when he became a specialist in crime.

It was a quarter past six when we left Baker Street, and it still wanted ten minutes to the hour when we found ourselves in Serpentine Avenue. It was already dusk, and the electric lamps were just igniting as we paced up and down in front of Briony Lodge, waiting for the coming of its occupant. The house was just such as I had pictured it from Sherlock Holmes' succinct description, but the locality appeared to be less private than I expected. On the contrary, for a small street in a quiet neighbourhood, it was remarkably animated. There was a group of shabbily dressed men smoking and laughing in a corner, a scissors-grinder with his wheel, two guardsmen who were flirting with a nurse-girl, and several well-dressed young men who were lounging up and down with cigars in their mouths.

"You see," remarked Holmes, as we paced to and fro in front of the house, "this marriage rather simplifies matters. The photograph becomes a double-edged weapon now. The chances are that she would be as averse to its being seen by Mr. Godfrey Norton, as our client is to its coming to the eyes of his princess. Now the question is—Where are we to find the photograph?"

"Where, indeed?"

"It is most unlikely that she carries it about with her. It is cabinet size. Too large for easy concealment about a woman's dress. She knows that the King is capable of having her waylaid and searched. Two attempts of the sort have already been made. We may take it, then, that she does not carry it about with her."

"Where, then?"

"Her banker or her lawyer. There is that double possibility. But I am inclined to think neither. Women are naturally secretive, and they like to do their own secreting. Why should she hand it over to anyone else? She could trust her own guardianship, but she could not tell what indirect or political influence might be brought to bear upon a business man. Besides, remember that she had resolved to use it within a few days. It must be where she can lay her hands upon it. It must be in her own house."

"But it has twice been burgled."

"Pshaw! They did not know how to look."

"But how will you look?"

"I will not look."

"What then?"

"I will get her to show me."

"But she will refuse."

"She will not be able to. But I hear the rumble of wheels. It is her carriage. Now carry out my orders to the letter."

As he spoke the gleam of the sidelights of a carriage came round the curve of the avenue. It was a smart little landau which rattled up to the door of Briony Lodge. As it pulled up, one of the loafing men at the corner dashed forward to open the door in the hope of earning a copper, but was elbowed away by another loafer, who had rushed up with the same intention. A fierce quarrel broke out, which was increased by the two guardsmen, who took sides with one of the loungers, and by the scissors-grinder, who was equally hot upon the other side. A blow was struck, and in an instant the lady, who had stepped from her carriage, was the centre of a little knot of flushed and struggling men, who struck savagely at each other with their fists and sticks. Holmes dashed into the crowd to protect the lady; but, just as he reached her, he gave a cry and dropped to the ground, with the blood running freely down his face. At his fall the guardsmen took to their heels in one direction and the loungers in the other, while a number of better dressed people,

who had watched the scuffle without taking part in it, crowded in to help the lady and to attend to the injured man. Irene Adler had hurried up the steps; but she stood at the top with her superb figure outlined against the lights of the hall, looking back into the street.

"Is the poor gentleman much hurt?" she asked.

"He is dead," cried several voices.

"No, no, there's life in him!" shouted another. "But he'll be gone before you can get him to hospital."

"He's a brave fellow," said a woman. "They would have had the lady's purse and watch if it hadn't been for him. They were a gang, and a rough one, too. Ah, he's breathing now."

"He can't lie in the street. May we bring him in, ma'am?"

"Surely. Bring him into the sitting-room. There is a comfortable sofa. This way, please!"

***

Slowly and solemnly Holmes was borne into Briony Lodge and laid out in the principal room, while I still observed the proceedings from my post by the window. The lamps had been lit, but the blinds had not been drawn, so that I could see Holmes as he lay upon the couch. I do not know whether he was seized with compunction at that moment for the part he was playing, but I know that I never felt more heartily ashamed of myself in my life than when I saw the beautiful creature against whom I was conspiring, or the grace and kindliness with which she waited upon the injured man. And yet it would be the blackest treachery to Holmes to draw back now from the part which he had intrusted to me. I hardened my heart, and took the smoke-rocket from under my ulster. After all, I thought, we are not injuring her. We are but preventing her from injuring another.

Holmes had sat up upon the couch, and I saw him motion like a man who is in need of air. A maid rushed across and threw open the window. At the same instant I saw him raise his hand and at the signal I tossed my rocket into the room with a cry of "Fire!" The word was no sooner out of my mouth than the whole crowd of spectators, well dressed and ill—gentlemen, ostlers, and servant maids—joined in a general shriek of "Fire!" Thick clouds of smoke curled through the room and out at the open window. I caught a glimpse of rushing figures, and a moment later the voice of Holmes from within assuring them that it was a false alarm. Slipping through the shouting crowd I made my way to the corner of the street, and in ten minutes was rejoiced to find my

friend's arm in mine, and to get away from the scene of uproar. He walked swiftly and in silence for some few minutes until we had turned down one of the quiet streets which lead towards the Edgeware Road.

"You did it very nicely, Doctor," he remarked. "Nothing could have been better. It is all right."

"You have the photograph?"

"I know where it is."

"And how did you find out?"

"She showed me, as I told you she would."

"I am still in the dark."

"I do not wish to make a mystery," said he, laughing. "The matter was perfectly simple. You, of course, saw that everyone in the street was an accomplice. They were all engaged for the evening."

"I guessed as much."

"Then, when the row broke out, I had a little moist red paint in the palm of my hand. I rushed forward, fell down, clapped my hand to my face, and became a piteous spectacle. It is an old trick."

"That also I could fathom."

"Then they carried me in. She was bound to have me in. What else could she do? And into her sitting-room, which was the very room which I suspected. It lay between that and her bedroom, and I was determined to see which. They laid me on a couch, I motioned for air,

they were compelled to open the window, and you had your chance."

"How did that help you?"

"It was all-important. When a woman thinks that her house is on fire, her instinct is at once to rush to the thing which she values most. It is a perfectly overpowering impulse, and I have more than once taken advantage of it. In the case of the Darlington Substitution Scandal it was of use to me, and also in the Arnsworth Castle business. A married woman grabs at her baby; an unmarried one reaches for her jewel-box. Now it was clear to me that our lady of to-day had nothing in the house more precious to her than what we are in quest of. She would rush to secure it. The alarm of fire was admirably done. The smoke and shouting were enough to shake nerves of steel. She responded beautifully. The photograph is in a recess behind a sliding panel just above the right bell-pull. She was there in an instant, and I caught a glimpse of it as she half drew it out. When I cried out that it was a false alarm, she replaced it, glanced at the rocket, rushed from the room, and I have not seen her since. I rose, and, making my excuses, escaped from the house. I hesitated whether to attempt to secure the photograph at once; but the coachman had come in, and as he was watching me narrowly, it seemed safer to wait. A little over-precipitance may ruin all."

"And now?" I asked.

"Our quest is practically finished. I shall call with the King tomorrow, and with you, if you care to come with us. We will be shown into the sitting-room to wait for the lady, but it is probable that when she comes she may find neither us nor the photograph. It might be a satisfaction to his Majesty to regain it with his own hands."

"And when will you call?"

"At eight in the morning. She will not be up, so that we shall have a clear field. Besides, we must be prompt, for this marriage may mean a complete change in her life and habits. I must wire to the King without delay."

***

We had reached Baker Street and had stopped at the door. He was searching his pockets for the key when someone passing said:

"Goodnight, Mister Sherlock Holmes."

There were several people on the pavement at the time, but the greeting appeared to come from a slim youth in an ulster who had hurried by.

"I've heard that voice before," said Holmes, staring down the dimly lit street. "Now, I wonder who the deuce that could have been."

III. Portrait of the Woman

I slept at Baker Street that night, and we were engaged upon our toast and coffee in the morning when the King of Bohemia, again disguised by his black vizard mask, rushed into the room.

"You have really got it!" he cried, grasping Sherlock Holmes by either shoulder and looking eagerly into his face.

"Not yet."

"But you have hopes?"

"I have hopes."

"Then, come. I am all impatience to be gone."

"We must have a cab."

"No, my Mannheim is waiting."

"Then that will simplify matters." We descended and started off once more for Briony Lodge.

"Irene Adler is married," remarked Holmes.

"Married! When?"

"Yesterday."

"But to whom?"

"To an English lawyer named Norton."

"But she could not love him."

"I am in hopes that she does."

"And why in hopes?"

"Because it would spare your Majesty all fear of future annoyance. If the lady loves her husband, she does not love your Majesty. If she does not love your Majesty, there is no reason why she should interfere with your Majesty's plan."

"It is true. And yet—! Well! I wish she had been of my own station! What a queen she would have made!" He relapsed into a moody silence, which was not broken until we drew up in Serpentine Avenue.

The door of Briony Lodge was open, and an elderly woman stood upon the steps. She watched us with a sardonic eye as we stepped from the motorized carriage.

"Mr. Sherlock Holmes, I believe?" said she.

"I am Mr. Holmes," answered my companion, looking at her with a questioning and rather startled gaze.

"Indeed! My mistress told me that you were likely to call. She left this morning with her husband by the 5:15 train from Charing Cross for the Continent."

"What!" Sherlock Holmes staggered back, white with chagrin and surprise. "Do you mean that she has left England?"

"Never to return."

"And the papers?" asked the King hoarsely. "All is lost."

"The papers?" Holmes repeated,

casting a curious glance toward me as he mounted the steps into Briony Lodge. "We shall see."

He pushed past the servant and rushed into the drawing-room, followed by the King and myself. The furniture was scattered about in every direction, with dismantled shelves and open drawers, as if the lady had hurriedly ransacked them before her flight. Holmes rushed at the bell-pull, tore back a small sliding shutter, and, plunging in his hand, pulled out a photograph and a letter. The photograph was of Irene Adler herself in evening dress, the letter was superscribed to "Sherlock Holmes, Esq. To be left till called for." My friend tore it open, and we all three read it together. It was dated at midnight of the preceding night and ran in this way:

"*MY DEAR MR. SHERLOCK HOLMES,—You really did it very well. You took me in completely. Until after the alarm of fire, I had not a suspicion. But then, when I found how I had betrayed myself, I began to think. I had been warned against you months ago. I had been told that, if the King employed an agent, it would certainly be you. And your address had been given me. Yet, with all this, you made me reveal what you wanted to know. Even after I became suspicious, I found it hard to think evil of such a dear, kind old clergyman. But, you know, I have been trained as an actress myself. Male costume is nothing new to me. I often take advantage of the freedom which it gives. I sent John, the coachman, to watch you, ran upstairs, got into my walking clothes, as I call them, and came down just as you departed.*

Well, I followed you to your door, and so made sure that I was really an object of interest to the celebrated Mr. Sherlock Holmes. Then I, rather imprudently, wished you good-night, and started for the Temple to see my husband.

We both thought the best resource was flight, when pursued by so formidable an antagonist; so you will find the nest empty when you call tomorrow. As to the photograph, your client may rest in peace. I love and am loved by a better man than he. The King may do what he will without hindrance from one whom he has cruelly wronged. I keep it only to safeguard myself, and to preserve a weapon which will always secure me from any steps which he might take in the future. I leave a photograph which he might care to possess; and I remain, dear Mr. Sherlock Holmes,

Very truly yours,

IRENE NORTON, ADLER."

***

"What a woman—oh, what a woman!" cried the King of Bohemia, when we had all three read this epistle. "Did I not tell you how quick and resolute she was? Would she not have made an admirable queen? Is it not a pity that she was not on my level?"

"From what I have seen of the lady, she seems, indeed, to be on a very different level to your Majesty," said Holmes coldly. "I am sorry that I have not been able to bring your Majesty's business to a more successful conclusion."

"On the contrary, my dear sir," cried the King after a brief pause; "nothing could be more successful. I know that her word is inviolate. The photograph is now as safe as if it were in the fire."

"I am glad to hear your Majesty say so."

"I am immensely indebted to you. Pray tell me in what way I can reward you. This ring—" He slipped an emerald snake ring from his finger and held it out upon the palm of his hand.

"Your Majesty has something which I should value even more highly," said Holmes.

"You have but to name it."

"This photograph!"

The King stared at him in amazement.

"Irene's photograph!" he cried.

"Certainly, if you wish it."

"I thank your Majesty. Then there is no more to be done in the matter. I have the honour to wish you a very good morning." He bowed, and, turning away without observing the hand which the King had stretched out to him, he set off in my company for his chambers.

"Is that it?" I asked once we had boarded a hansom. "I can't help feeling I've missed something."

"As have I, Watson." Holmes examined the cabinet card and the glass frame in which it was mounted. Removing the pins he opened up the back to examine it in more detail. "I am to infer that this photograph was taken yesterday afternoon, en route to St. Monica's. See the name on the reverse? I foolishly mistook it for a jewellers."

The ornate scroll-work proclaimed it to be from the photographic studio of Gross & Hankey in Regent Street.

"A photographer is as relevant to a wedding as a jeweller, Holmes."

"Had a photographer been in attendance, I should not have been needed as a witness Watson; and what bride reflects upon her wedding day by taking a photograph without the groom being present?"

"What are you saying Holmes?"

"That the wedding was a sham—a distraction. Miss Adler herself admits to being warned about me even

before my services were procured, and then there were the papers the King referred to."

"The letters you mean."

"No, my friend. The documents concerned were not love letters, just as the photograph was in all likelihood not one of a compromising nature. There is no way the King would hold the word of a blackmailer as inviolate, nor would he be keen to accompany an agent to recover something so publicly, masked or otherwise."

"What then?"

"What indeed", said he, ordering the cabman to divert to Regent Street.

IV. The Missing Clue

The entrance to Gross & Sankey was not as we had expected, and not an easy place to find. Holmes pressed the bell, pausing briefly to examine the brass plate fixed to the terraced doorway. It was certainly no jewellers, but a private photographic studio situated in a first floor apartment.

"I pride myself in having an exact knowledge of London, Watson, and when it comes to streets and businesses I have the same grounding in the knowledge as any experienced cabman, yet the name Gross & Sankey is not familiar to me. Had I consulted my Index I am certain I would not have found it. The plaque here is untarnished, with new screws. I suspect very few cabmen in London would yet know of it."

"What are you suggesting?"

"Miss Adler's coachman, John, was in her employ. There is no way she could travel here by landau, have her photograph taken, and then ride on to St. Monica's to arrive there before me; and besides, she wore her hair more neatly in this photograph than she did yesterday, for when she posed she was in no hurry; she also had no parasol."

"A ruse then," said I as a young boy, the photographer's assistant, allowed us inside and escorted us up the stairs.

"One which preceded our own."

***

Entering the studio, we were greeted by a short, middle-aged gentleman whom I took to be in his early fifties. He was balding, bespectacled and smartly dressed in a black suit and tie.

Ushering us inside and dismissing his assistant, the photographer led us through into the rear of the apartment, which was flooded with strong light through a set of large undraped windows. There were a number of old tea chests filled with costumes and photographic props scattered around, and a classic chaise longue sat at one end of the room. At the other stood a draped booth set up for portraiture. In the centre were a trestle table, three chairs, two studio cameras and several reflector screens.

"Herr Gross? My name is Sherlock Holmes, as you may already be aware. When did you take this photograph?"

Unfazed by my friend's abrupt interrogation, the gentleman gave a nod of acknowledgement. He took the cabinet and adjusted his pince-nez to examine the card in more detail.

"I took this yesterday," he said in a clipped German accent. "Fräulein Adler came by at a quarter to twelve."

"Did she indeed?" Holmes added, surveying the room. "If that were so, it would have been to collect the picture, not to have it taken."

"You are mistaken..."

"I think not," said Holmes, indicating an empty plate box on the trestle table. "I see you prepare several photographic plates at a time. Enough to take four or six pictures? Plus you need to refill your powder flash between takes. That would take more time than Fräulein Adler could possibly have had.

"Not at all. I am a fast worker, Herr Holmes."

"Very fast, I should think, for you are not fully unpacked from your recent relocation, and much of your equipment is not readily to hand; or are you saying that she came here to have a single photograph taken?"

"Alone, yes." Gross confirmed, "I took only the one picture."

"So you did not meet her husband-to-be. Nor do you recall that she should now be known as Frau Norton?"

"Ja, of course," the man was clearly flustered. "I forget this. I only ever knew her as Adler."

"I would advise you never to make up answers on the spot, Herr Gross, for I will always find you out. I observe a mix of old daguerreotypes, recently smudged by smoke damage, much like your packing crates," Holmes indicated the tea chests, "and your brand new studio cameras are barely used."

Holmes crossed the room to the draped booth, where he examined a parasol that rested there. Upon seeing it, Her Gross became quite agitated.

"You should leave," said he, urgently. "You have no business intruding upon me like this."

"I am not here to harass you Herr Gross," said Holmes, dismissing the protest with a wave of his hand, "merely to determine the facts of a case I am working upon."

Holmes returned his attention to the studio cameras and the trestle table, where he slid aside the empty plate box that rested there. He then picked up a printed pamphlet that lay beneath. It was an advertisement for a D'Oyly Carte double bill being staged at the Savoy Theatre.

"You are a fan of opera, Herr Gross?"

"What of it?"

"I thought not," he said brusquely,

"but I note from your accent that you are a Bohemian. I suspect it is more than coincidence that the case started with a picture taken in Bohemia, and that the photographer who takes the new picture is also a Bohemian. I am willing to entertain the suggestion that it was you who took the original, and that you were forced to flee to England with the negative plates."

"It is true," said Gross, slumping into one of the chairs. "I came here to avoid persecution and my troubles have followed me."

"Persecution by the Grand Duke?"

"Just so. As you say, I was employed to take private photographs at court, and when a Royal courtship loomed, I was instructed to destroy my work."

"You refused?"

Gross shook his head. "Before I was able to do it, the King's men came and started to ransack my studio in Karlsbad. They were interrupted by men with guns, who killed them before spiriting me away with my equipment. The plates were not so lucky. Within a month I was here, in London, setting up a new studio with Herr Sankey, who has himself relocated from Brixton."

"These men, why did they help you?"

"I do not know them, Herr Holmes, but I assumed that Fräulein Adler was involved."

"It seems unlikely that Miss Adler could furnish you enough resources to set up thousands of miles from home. Were you given any warnings?"

"Only by Fräulein Adler. She warned me that you would come here yesterday, before she fled the country. She told me you were an agent of the King."

"Yesterday I was acting on his behalf, and that matter is concluded. Today I am set to find out on whose behalf I am acting. Mine, the King's, or Miss Adler's. One last question, Herr Gross, and you must forgive me for asking. Was the photograph of an intimate nature?"

"I am a respectable photographer! It is true that the King was something of a rogue where women were concerned, but he never made that kind of request. It is also true that he and Miss Adler were lovers, but the photograph showed only a shared kiss in a public place."

"Do you recall the town and the purpose of the visit there?"

"Of course, St. Joachimsthal, in the shadow of the Ore mountains. The King was on an official visit to celebrate its rebuilding in the wake of a fire some years ago."

"So, public officials were present?"

"Ja," Gross nodded.

"Were there any in the photograph?"

"There would have been, but I cannot say who."

"You've said enough, Herr Gross. Come, Watson, we have no further business here."

***

In our hansom Holmes shared the theatre pamphlet with me. It announced a Savoy operetta, Mrs. Jarramie's Genie, and a production of Gilbert & Sullivan's comic opera H.M.S. Pinafore.

"You will recall, Watson, that Miss Adler is formerly an operatic contralto."

"I do, but what of it?"

"This is doubtless how she came to meet the King. Herr Gros, on the other hand, was clearly not a follower of opera. It has been my experience that photographers with a love of such things acquire properties that reflect their interest. Being pictured in the the regalia of a Papageno or a Parsifal seems to be quite a popular pastime, yet I saw no theatrical costume, just outfits and properties used for formal portraiture."

I was comforted to see that my friend's deductions were now coming thick and fast, and that any dark mood precipitated by thoughts of failure had been curtailed.

"Miss Adler did not pose for photographs yesterday, but did so very recently. The parasol retained the same perfume that I observed. I also spied a pair of opera tickets set upon her mantelpiece. I believe they corresponded to these performances."

"Then she is still in London?"

"Indeed Watson, and doubtless she will remain in hiding until the matter is resolved. It should be a small matter for me to determine which day she will visit the Savoy."

"Will she not be using an assumed name?" I smiled, pointing out the obvious.

"She may well be, but her unfinished business is with the Grand Duke, and it must be resolved before his betrothal is announced two days hence. I have no doubt that she plans to attend on the very same evening that Count Von Kramm has arranged to take a box."

"How can you be so sure, Holmes?"

"The vizard mask, Watson. The King stands well above six feet tall and seems to have no concept of blending in to disguise himself. He is used to wearing a mask at social functions either to avoid being disturbed or to excuse his rather questionable morality. He referred to Miss Adler as an adventuress, but he might as well have been calling her a courtesan, for that is how he views her. It seems most likely that they met during her La Scala tour, which I have since confirmed played in Mannheim, a city favoured by Bohemian music-lovers and the very place where his Majesty would have acquired his motorized carriage."

V. A Night at the Operetta

Holmes returned to Baker Street alone, set upon discovering the purpose of the Grand Duke's visit to England, while I returned to Mrs Watson. I had little choice but to confess that I was once again involved in a case with Holmes, and that I was bound to see it through. She was far from happy with the idea which, she was at pains to remind me, was in direct violation of our marital arrangements. I spent a sleepless night my surgery armchair before leaving early to avoid any further debate.

Holmes and I met again at ten the next morning, where I found him quite alert and pacing up and down the floor of his chamber, a cloud of blue cigarette smoke trailed behind him. I immediately recognised the smell of cannabis and took note of his untouched breakfast at table. The events of the previous day were clearly playing on his mind, and I could only conclude that he too had had a sleepless night, turning to the drug as a means of keeping him alert during a night of heavy research. Restraining myself from any comment (for I had not seen him indulge in the midst of a case before) I considered the consequences of failure.

"Come, Watson, sit! Sit!"

I took a seat in my comfortable old armchair to play audience to Holmes' revelations.

"I am forced, in the absence of facts, to rely upon theory," said Holmes with candid irony. "First we have Grand Duke Wilhelm, the King of Bohemia. A man who, when he is about to be married, orders compromising images to be destroyed. He then drives from Prague to London to protect his reputation by accusing Miss Adler of blackmail, yet when she reassures him of her integrity he acquiesces quickly and agrees to let the matter lie. His infatuation with the woman is obvious, as is his snobbery; but it is also clear that there is another, darker aspect to this blackmail."

"We know that Miss Adler and Herr Gross both have a mysterious benefactor unafraid of using criminal force to protect his secret. This same benefactor wants the photograph for himself, but the woman has integrity. She will not part with it for either party. This leads me to conclude that it is not Miss Adler that threatened the King, but her saviour."

"But who is this saviour?"

"Someone in the photograph. For just as Miss Adler's testimony would only be believed by such evidence, so too would the testimony of any other accuser. So a businessman or public official with the means to call upon armed thugs would seem to be our villain, and I have the very culprit."

"You do?"

"Professor James Moriarty."

"Again?" I sighed, for the man always seemed to be involved, yet always sat beyond our grasp. "Why would it be he?"

"The town of St. Joachimsthal was home to one of the most well-known silver and iron mines on the Continent until, when the mine started to run dry, the people started to drift away. Being state run, the mine became a drain on its resources, but salvation came, most unexpectedly, when three quarters of the town mysteriously burned to the ground in March of '73. The belief is that fires set in the mines may have been responsible. The mine closed and was sold on to new interests, who rebuilt it and now, it seems, have made the mine profitable once more. Instead of silver they mine a variety of newly identified minerals including something called pitchblende, whose properties are of great interest to scientists and engineers all across the world."

"And these new interests?"

"In 1871 a holding company took majority shares in a coal mining company to whom, two years later, Crown Prince Wilhelm transferred certain mining interests. The company was renamed Gewerkschaft Mariasorg, making its headquarters in an old Capuchin monastery that overlooks St. Joachimsthal. The chairman of its board is none other than James Moriarty."

"Remarkable,"

"Elementary. There will of course be no way to directly connect the Professor to this affair without the photograph in Miss Adler's possession, and protecting her interests is the best way to

gain access to it."

"Which brings me to the lawyer, Godfrey Norton."

"Yes," said I. "I had wondered about him. If he is not married to Miss Adler, what is his role in all of this?"

"Consider, Watson. Norton is a successful member of the Middle Temple with impeccable credentials. He is dashing, has an unblemished record, is well-mannered and no doubt popular with the ladies. Quite the catch to an ordinary woman, but this woman," he paused to consider, "this adventuress who turns the heads of Royalty and runs rings around their various agents? He is just the sort of man she would employ to act on her behalf."

I shook my head. "To what end Holmes?"

"To extricate her from this mess, Watson. The King is bent on retrieving the document by any means necessary. While the photograph keeps Miss Adler alive, she will be forced to hide until the matter is settled. I suspect that Norton tried to negotiate, but that my assignment by the King was an attempt to avoid such complications. By outwitting me she has forced a deal back on the table, and the Savoy is where it shall be struck."

"And Moriarty?" I asked. "If you are right he'll not sit idly by while she betrays him."

"Moriarty has a more subtle agenda. It was he who brought Gross to England, he who warned Miss Adler of my involvement, and doubtless it was he who engineered my own involvement. These events were set as a lure to bring the Grand Duke here, to England."

"For what purpose?"

"The photograph has no value if the King is dead, an in the current climate a Royal death on British soil could have untold consequences. Wilhelm may be the hereditary King of Bohemia, but he does not rule it. I must conclude that the King is in mortal danger, and that he is to be assassinated as he attends the opera with Miss Adler this very night!"

***

The events of that evening passed quickly. Since we last shared rooms, Holmes had elected to install one of the new wireless Teslagraphs that were flooding the market. The idea that high-speed messages can be transmitted, without cables, from home to office still astounds me as does much of the technology taking a hold of the city. Holmes settled down to encode two messages, one for Scotland Yard, and another to the Langham Hotel. He then disappeared to prepare his disguise for the evening.

I, meanwhile, procured a private box, courtesy of the King's fees, set on the same balcony as his own. I had with me my medical bag, which Holmes suggested I bring should things go wrong. I also carried with me my service revolver, which I had chosen to conceal within my bag.

I arrived at seven thirty with a simple plan. I was to be alert and to look for any possible assassin, giving an alarm if anything should occur. The crowds were not too dense, for the evening's performances were not new, though the Savoy was popular enough. The first performance, the operetta, was scheduled to start at eight, and would attract a much smaller audience, while for Pinafore, at nine, the numbers were sure to swell.

Try as I might, I could not see Holmes in the crowd. I had left before his disguise was complete, and had no idea what to look for, though I was alert for any jostling that might occur should he relieve me of the spare ticket that I carried in my trouser pocket. Nor could I see any sign of Miss Adler, although I spied one or two Scotland Yarders cautiously perusing the theatregoers. Avoiding their attentions, I moved into the foyer where, shortly before the curtain was due to rise, the Count Von Kramm's party arrived. I did not see him enter, but when a Bohemian officer passed me by in the crowd, I realised that Grand Duke Wilhelm must also be taking precautions.

From my seat in the upper balcony I could see that the King was occupying the Royal box. As he had during his visits to Baker Street, he wore the black vizard mask, although from his great frame I could be absolutely certain it was the same man. Accompanying him that night were a bureaucrat of some sort, an army officer, and, as Holmes had predicted, Irene Adler and the young moustachioed gentleman that I presumed to be the lawyer, Godfrey Norton.

I scanned the theatre anxiously, working out the best vantage points from which an assassin might emerge, but I saw nothing. After the play was in progress, a figure stepped into the box. It was a second Bohemian officer —the one I had seen in the foyer. There was a brief exchange before the officer took a seat, and the King resumed his discussions with his former mistress.

What happened next was a blur. From the corner of my eye I spied some movement, high up and to the left of the stage. As Holmes feared, it was the barrel of a rifle protruding between the framing curtain and the stage wall.

I stood, fumbling with my bag as I attempted to retrieve my service revolver, while at the same time shouting out and pointing towards the killer.

It was too late. There was a brief flash as the assassin fired, and then the rifle was out of view. I had my service revolver in my hand, and could perceive screams from the audience in the pits as the performance below came to a halt. A brief glance towards the Royal box showed chaos. The King was slumped forward while Miss Adler appeared to be holding him, trying, no doubt, to revive him.

The evil deed was done, and my priority was not to give pursuit to the assassin, but to render immediate assistance to the King, if he yet survived.

***

Having only been three boxes from the Royal party, I was first on the scene, quickly followed by the police. Barging past Norton and the bureaucrat, I was soon seated at the King's table where I assessed the situation. I lifted the King's head to examine where the bullet had struck, and in an instant realised that he was alive and only dazed. There was a neat hole in the centre of the mask, between the eyes, but there was no sign of blood. As I began to slide back the vizard mask I met with some resistance, and realized that a second mask, of metal plate, lay beneath.

It was that very same moment that Miss Adler slumped forward, dislodged by my ministrations. Her face crashed onto the table, upon which lay the photograph and a pile of letters. I watched helplessly as a bloody stain spread across them, obscuring forever the heart of the matter.

VI. The Sealed Letter

It was not until close to midnight that Holmes and I were reunited. He was, as is often the case in the wake of an investigation, filled with manic energy.

"The King is well?"

"In fine health," I confirmed, reluctant to divulge anything further until he had expended himself upon the telling of our adventure's conclusion.

"I had suspected that the vizard mask had a third purpose, and knowing an assassin's aim might be true, I was assured that he was in little danger. Our exchange was brief, for I had forwarded my suspicions to the Langham, and of my intention to assume the guise of a Bohemian guardsman. Like you, I failed to see the assassin until the very last moment, when the killer's rifle was discharged. I heard no sound until the bullet ricocheted from the iron mask concealed beneath the vizard.

"I heard no sound either," said I, "for I realised very quickly that the killer's rifle was of the sort used by a unit of sharpshooters I had encountered in Afghanistan."

"The First Air Rifles? Yes, a first class observation, Watson. I've long suspected that some of their number were active as assassins-for-hire. I was unable to examine the weapon myself as the killer had fled by the time I reached his perch on the gridiron above the stage. He was quite an able fellow, crossing overhead like the Great Blondin to the other side. You may not be aware, Watson, but as a child I was privileged to observe Blondin prepare for his Niagara crossing in no less a place than Birmingham, where a practice wire was set across the local reservoir. I too was therefore to mount the gridiron in pursuit of the man, and I believe I made up some distance as he reached a ladder to the roof set against the far wall. As I followed him through the hatch and onto the roof, I realised that he had accomplices, and that the escape had been well-prepared."

"Like many of the taller buildings in London, the Savoy had had sodium spotlights and an aerostat mooring post installed, usually accessible from the other side of the building, and a small aerostat waited some thirty feet above as the killer mounted a hanging ladder. Thankfully the spots illuminated it well, and I recorded the registration even as the men on

board took pot-shots at me from the gondola. These too would have been air rifles, I am sure, as the only sound was that of bullets bouncing off brickwork and the occasional metal fitting. The concentration of their fire kept my head low—these were trained sharpshooters, after all—until the ship cast off and they were heading southeast, towards Southwark."

"I was reluctant to trade shots and bring the crashing dirigible down onto the Strand, so I ran to the edge, looking for the best means of pursuit. And there it was, parked to the rear of the Savoy. The King's Mannheim-Benz."

"Good lord Holmes," said I, secretly a little miffed that Holmes had been having all the fun while I had been left to deal with all the drama, "you stole his carriage?"

"Borrowed, Watson. I found a ladder to descend and then, using a technique I learned whilst disguised as a navy tar, I placed my insteps on either side of the metal ladder, sliding downwards at great speed. I did catch my ankles several times but did no lasting damage, although I was forced to hobble across the few yards that separated me from the Mannheim."

"I had no idea you could drive, Holmes."

"Nor I, Watson, but I have observed, and my recollection of the ignition procedure was flawless.

Within moments I was on the Strand and heading East towards Waterloo Bridge. The right turn was quite hair-raising as I was travelling at speed—well above thirty miles per hour, and I soon had the aerostat in my sight. I pursued them through Walworth and Peckham towards Bromley, at which point I was confident that a firearm could be used to bring them down."

"You shot them?"

Holmes shook his head. "I tried, but again the sharpshooters kept me at bay, splintering the front window and forcing me to leave the road at one point. By the time I had recovered control of the carriage, they had gained sufficient altitude to be out of my range, and I was forced to call off the chase."

"So they got away?"

"I'm afraid so," said Holmes, "but we're playing the long game here. The evidence against Moriarty is mounting and one day soon I shall be able to prove, beyond any doubt, his criminal pedigree. At least the King and Miss Adler are safe, and the photographs?"

He looked at me and at the expression upon my face. I am perhaps the easiest of people to read, and for Holmes such things are second nature. He knew immediately that things did not go as well as he had hoped.

"You did recover the photograph?"

I nodded. "I fear it is of little use now, however. The blood you see..."

The colour drained from my companion's face, and any suggestion that he might eschew emotion in favour of pure logic was, for a moment at least, cast aside.

"And Miss Adler?"

"It was the ricochet, Holmes. The bullet struck her in the temple."

"I see," he turned away from me then, so I could only imagine the expression upon his face. Then, reaching into my tweed, I withdrew a sealed letter, similar in all respects to that he had received the preceding afternoon. This time the superscription simply read "Sherlock Holmes, Esq.", but in all other respects it looked the same. Upon opening it, Holmes noted there was no date, and began to read aloud.

"MY DEAR MR. SHERLOCK HOLMES,—I am hoping that, as you are reading this, I am long gone. By now you will have realised that dear Godfrey is just my lawyer and not my husband, and that my deceptions were necessary to reconcile my position with the King. I was present when you called upon Herr Gross, and I could tell from your conclusions that you and your companion are both men of integrity.

I doubt that our paths shall cross again, for I shall very shortly assume a new life and a new identity which shall, I am sure, place me beyond even your considerable powers of detection.

As to the King, he is not such a scoundrel as you may assume. Our romance, while brief, was conducted at the same time that his marriage was being arranged, and the wrong that he did to me was to do his duty rather than to follow his infatuation. I shall always remain, my dear Mr. Sherlock Holmes,

Very truly yours,

IRENE ADLER."

"One step ahead, Watson," he said at last. "Had she not been, perhaps she would be alive today."

And that was how a great scandal threatened to affect the kingdom of Bohemia, and how the best plans of Mr. Sherlock Holmes were beaten by a woman's wit. He used to make merry over the cleverness of women, but I have not heard him do it of late. And when he speaks of the late Irene Adler, or when he refers to her photograph, it is always under the honourable title of the woman.

EPILOGUE

From the Medical Journal of John H. Watson M.D.
—23rd March, 1888.

Tonight I must wrestle with my conscience as the dictates of my Hippocratic oath conflict with my relationship with my good friend, Sherlock Holmes.

The oath states that "Whatever, in connection with my professional service, or not in connection with it, I see or hear, in the life of men, which ought not to be spoken of abroad, I will not divulge, as reckoning that all such should be kept secret."

The moment I administered professional medical aid to Miss Irene Adler, the needs of doctor-patient confidentiality took precedence over my working relationship with Holmes. On the orders of the King of Bohemia, the box in which Miss Adler sustained her injured was cleared, and I set about my work.

The bullet wound was bloody, but minor, having severed a temporal arteriole on Miss Adler's left temple and rendered her unconscious. Whether this was from the impact or the loss of blood I was uncertain, but I took advantage of her condition to stitch the wound and apply a dressing. After several minutes, with the application of sal volatile, I was able to rouse her and examine her responses. As she recovered, the King sought reassurance that Miss Adler would survive. I confirmed this, but suggested close monitoring over the coming weeks in case of aneurysm.

At this point the King promised to look after Miss Adler, but added that the world must believe her dead, for "there are parties out there who will not brook betrayal". I realise of course that this was a veiled reference to Professor Moriarty, and I offered my assurance that neither Holmes nor I would divulge information about Miss Adler's condition or her whereabouts.

It was at this point that Miss Adler intervened. Placing her hand upon my arm, she echoed the King's words.

"Nobody must know," she said. "Not Mr. Holmes, not Godfrey. Nobody. You must promise me that. If I am to make a new life for myself only you, and Willi, and myself must know the truth."

I opened my mouth to protest, but thought better of it. My duty here was to the patient, not to my friend, and if even half of what Holmes had concluded about Moriarty turned out to be true, then retribution would be swift, and final.

I gave my word. From this day forward only the three people that were present in that theatre box shall know the truth, although I suspect that Holmes will deduce it of his own accord, given time and, of course, facts.

A NOTE ON PLACEMENT

The Great Game, in which Sherlockians piece together the clues laid down in Doyle's writing to work out where, and when, each of the sixty stories of the original canon occur, and to extrapolate—from clues laid down in the original texts—events that happen off the page, from Watson's wounds and marriages to the family and background of Holmes, Watson and Professor Moriarty.

Sometimes we are told the exact date on which a case begins, and sometimes there is not so much as a day or month mentioned. Worse, given dates do not always match those of a real calendar, and we must turn to behaviours, events and assumptions to come up with a coherent chronology. For many it is an impossible, unsolvable puzzle, finding consolation in the essays and deduction made by those that have gone before, such as Ronald Knox's Studies in the Literature of Sherlock Holmes, William S Baring-Gould's The Annotated Sherlock Holmes, and Leslie S Klinger's The New Annotated Sherlock Holmes. Of course, for the reimagining of the canon we have been able to consult and reference all of these, and also the various fictional biographies of Holmes from Vincent Starrett to Nick Rennison.

We also have the opportunity to cheat. By editing the original stories and adding new information as we progress, we can firm up the way that events have occurred in our own steampunk version of Holmes' life, but to do so we needed a starting point. We needed a readily available body of deductions that gave us enough information to consider each story on its own merits, and settled upon an online resource: The Sherlock Peoria's Chronology Corner established and maintained by Brad 'Birlstone Railway Smash' Keefauver. This proved an invaluable—if controversial—resource, which has allowed us to slowly piece together the story we want to tell, often straying from his deductions in favour of storytelling.

So, The Scoundrel of Bohemia? Whither does it fit? As the first story, A Scandal in Bohemia is perhaps the most fixed point in the original canon, with a bold statement from Watson that the case began on the 20th of March, 1888. As the establishing story we see this as an anchor, supported by Irene Adler's own background.

THEATRE OF JUDGEMENT

by Adrian Middleton

It may seem strange to consider that I, as a Welsh minister, might serve to document the deeds of my companion, but my narrative has become a matter of posterity. The circumstances of our meeting notwithstanding, it was not until we travelled into another time that the man's true nature was revealed to me. The nature of our meeting, and of our journeys along the fourth dimension, shall be recounted elsewhere. In this account I shall focus only upon the events of our arrival in the early summer of 1856, and of our encounter with the people of that time.

There was no thunder or lightning recorded over London for that fateful night. The Rookery of St. Giles was abuzz with the sound of footsteps and the indecipherable murmur of its evening trades—drunks engaging with prostitutes, labourers returning to the confines of their communal courts after a late day of work, and carousers meandering between dimly lit back yards and the public houses and beer shops that stood on every street corner. Thieves and rogues passed among them, dipping, coining, sharping, brawling— anything to turn a dishonest profit at the expense of their neighbours. The slums, packed to the rafters with Irish migrants, had a gang of hooligans on every street, and the recent brutality of their territorial battles had left only the desperate and the stupid to venture out onto the cobbles.

Michael Gahagan had been one of the first to notice it. Later accounts said that the street itself appeared to vibrate at short intervals, like the rippling of a hammer striking metal. Faster and faster it had come, slipping from intermittent thumps to a loud but steady bass vibration that crawled along the cobbles and up into the very bones of those present. The witnesses paused from their distractions, turning blindly in a desperate attempt to locate the source of the strange buzzing rumble. Around them, every fragile brick vibrated, and small clouds of crumbling mortar filled the night air in much the same way as coal-dust in the daytime, making it impossible to determine from whence the disturbance had come.

Then it happened. From the corner of his eye Gahagan had caught a

bright flicker coming from the old Three Ton Alley. It hadn't officially been called that since they had levelled the area beyond to make way for New Oxford Street, but to those who lived in the Rookery, the name had stuck. It was in the oldest part of St. Giles-in-the-Fields, where old Empress Maude's leper hospital once stood. Reaching into his breeches, Gahagan had felt the reassuring weight of his cosh, perhaps cursing that he wasn't better armed; but then he had a reputation as a brawler, and most of the carousers in these parts gave him a wide berth .

Passing along the dim street, Gahagan came to what was normally a black, featureless court, dilapidated and desperate for repair or demolition. It had been an adjunct to the old Rat's Castle, made derelict by changes to the area, but on this occasion its courtyard overflowed with brilliant light. Through unrepaired holes in the walls and roof he saw beams of blue-white light thrusting into the sky, piercing the chinks and fissures that lay between dislodged tiles and badly fitted shutters. Above the building's silhouette, caught in the light of the moon, a cloud of unearthly blue and yellow dust rose skywards, evicting the bats and starlings that fled the scene as a crowd of spectators began to gather.

Gahagan and several other men—whether brave or curious I remain unsure—came together, fronting the old court where they cast aside the shabby barricades that blocked their path. Passing through until they were surrounded by three walls, their path was made clear by a single moss-covered stone archway—much older than the surrounding buildings—that shed such light as burned into their eyes. While the others chose to shy away, Gahagan held his hand in front of his face to shield him from the warming light, before plunging inside. The dust-filled air cooled as he crossed the threshold, and the humming began to subside until he risked an open glance down into the building. The archway led not into apartments, as any other courtyard door would have done, but down into a narrow corridor enclosed by old yellow bricks that looked more like those of an old castle vault than the cheap clay bricks of a poorly built slum. Descending into darkness, the vault analogy doubtless came back to haunt him as the stairs ended with what could only be described as a medieval portcullis.

The rusted iron grille filled the corridor, its lower end submerged in dark stagnant water that cast dappled shadows onto the walls. Beyond the grate, flickers of dim-

light were scattered by ripples of water—something was moving.

***

The whine of rotating discs abated and the last flickers of electricity discharged themselves into the darkness, dancing over the water and illuminating the dust-filled chamber. At the heart of the room a large platform, part machine and part sled, rested awkwardly across the surface the pool. Four feet wide by twelve long, it bore a passing resemblance to a snow sled, resting on long metal runners that curved upwards ornately. The front of the device, behind a protective shield fitted with glowing lamps and brass metalwork, housed a central column and handles, with the padded two-person seat set behind it. The centre of the platform held the engine—a series of slowly rotating discs that discharged sparks into a transformer, while the rear was a flat-bed cart on which our cargo—covered and tied down with a tarred canvas—rested.

In the dim glow of the electrostatic discharge, I familiarised myself with our surroundings. Were it not for the water, the mouldy tide-marked walls and the absence of oil lamps, I would have declared that it matched the exact chamber we had departed from only moments earlier.

Rising from the platform, I caught our electrically distorted reflection in the water: two dark, insect like figures made sinister by our strange clothes. We each wore similar costumes: long black coats, vulcanised gloves, black boots and a purpose-made mask that combined protective goggles with a complex breathing apparatus that enveloped our mouths and noses. These masks were connected by thin tubes to small oxygen cylinders attached to the dark webbing harnesses that fitted over our coats.

Reaching up to remove my mask, I recoiled as my first breath took in the foetid air that filled the chamber.

"Good lord, it stinks," I remarked, stifling a retch as I fought to control my breathing. As I pulled the mask from my head my fingers briefly settled upon the signature accessory of my profession: a dog collar.

To the right, my taller companion adjusted the speed of the electrostatic dynamo, diverting power to the pair of large incandescent lanterns fixed at the front of the sled. As the room slowly filled with yellow light, he slipped his own mask away to reveal his high, domed forehead and sharp, penetrating features. He was a man of middle age, gaunt, and, based upon the manner in which he surveyed the chamber, somewhat sinister.

"That would be the sewers, reverend," he said dispassionately. "London is still afflicted by the Great

Stink, and it seems that I did not anticipate the higher water table. A few inches more water and we would have been poached."

"I don't like this, professor," I said, still suffering the after-effects of the journey. "These are dark forces you're messing with."

"Dark forces?" My companion smiled thinly, taking up his silver-topped cane before stepping from the sled and into the ankle-deep water. "I suppose that's an improvement on talk of the divine. I would have thought the things we have seen would have changed your perspective by now. For all its beauty, the universe is nothing more than the elegant numerical outcome of a stochastic process; a random construct."

I shook my head at the words. "Your numbers are beyond me..."

"And yet my numbers created the miracle that brought us here. Instead of interpreting superstitious texts you should have mastered your algebra. Mathematics helps us to understand the patterns of the cosmos, and with that knowledge change can be effected."

At that moment a disembodied voice echoed around the chamber.

"Who's there?" It was an Irish accent, more pronounced than my companion's, suggesting a lower class. I placed it as northern Irish, and determined that it had come from

outside—above us. The professor turned to me, pressing a slender finger to his lips and ushering me to investigate whilst slipping his other hand into one of his pockets.

Stepping down from the sled, I plunged into the icy water and cautiously waded across the chamber towards the source of the voice—an arched stone recess in the far corner of the room. The stone slabs were slippery with sludge, and I found myself using both the side of the sled, and then the walls, to steady myself until I reached my destination. Here I could see the small grille ahead, and the silhouette of the lanky Irishman that stood beyond.

"Who wants to know?" I asked.

"The name's Gahagan... father," he said. There was caution in his tone, but his voice seemed confident and without malice. "It's a heck of a commotion you're creating down here. What's going on?"

There had been no agreed explanation, and I was unused to thinking on my feet in such situations. As I opened my mouth to speak, my companion spoke for us.

"Michael Gahagan, is it?" He said. Incredulous, I turned to see that he had set aside his walking stick and was consulting a small pocketbook, like a Jewish broker reckoning his debts. Thumbing through his notes, he quickly settled on a page midway

through the book. "I know you."

The look on the Irishman's face changed into one of caution, and suspicion.

"How so?" He asked.

"You came to London... what? Six or seven years ago. Shortly after the Battle of Dolly's Brae? A Ribbonist if I recall correctly."

I could see Gahagan's face fall at being so discovered. The professor has the uncanny ability to use what knowledge he has to exert power over those around him, and to see him do it so casually sent a shiver down my spine.

I was later to learn that Gahagan had told no-one of his troubles in Ireland, and that his foolish decision to fire a shot into the air had started a battle that ended with six of his countrymen dead. Ostracised in his home town of Magheramayo, he had fled the taunts of his homeland and tried to lose himself in the slums of Holborn.

"Who are you? How would you know that?"

"The name is Moriarty," the professor smiled, his reptilian eyes unwavering as he locked his gaze upon the Irishman, "and I make it my business to know these things. Let him in, reverend, he's a decent lad, he can be trusted."

"Trusted?" Gahagan spat the word out.

I stood aside to let them speak, glancing at my companion whose own unblinking eyes gave nothing away. Gahagan, however, chose to break the gaze and turn his own eyes upon me. "The father here is a Protestant?"

The venom in the words was transparent, and I almost flushed with embarrassment as I realised that I might be seen as a greater threat than my godless companion.

"Welsh non-conformist as it happens," I said defensively.

"You see?" Moriarty smiled coldly. "Religion just creates conflict, reverend. Come inside, Michael, the father here is a gentle soul, you'll get no conflict from him. In fact, this is holy ground. Why don't you come inside, and let us show you."

***

As I drew down the thick length of chain suspended from the ceiling, the rusty grille slowly lifted out of the stagnant water. Gahagan remained wary. The flashing lights and the rumblings noises may have subsided, but his caution was tangible. If the presence of a protestant minister didn't unsettle him, the calm menace of the professor's words certainly did.

"Come in, come in," Moriarty said in an inviting and soft-spoken voice. "Careful of the water."

Passing me by, Gahagan took deep, shallow breaths, minimising the impact of the foul stench as he took long and cautious steps into the rank water. As he peered into the chamber I could see his eyes settle on the strange tilted contraption that had brought us from the future.

"What is that thing?" And what is it you're doing down here? We all know each other in these parts, but I've never seen either of you—"

"That thing is a device we are working on, Mr Gahagan," said the professor. "It was a little bit... noisier than we intended. Cheap rent is always a consideration, and we've only recently arrived. Is there a problem?"

Gahagan eyed the sled like a man eyeing a prize. It was an intricate construct, and I could see the greed in his eyes as he evaluated the scrap value of the brass rods and quartz components. Settling on our cargo, he stepped up and reached forwards, his attempt foiled by the swift downward sweep of Moriarty's cane, whipping against the canvas only inches ahead of his fingers.

"You are paid to protect the local coiners, are you not?" the professor asked sharply. "Is there any reason why you might not be similarly employed to protect my interests?"

"Aye," said Gahagan, cautiously, "but why wouldn't I just take what I want now, and make more money

from fencing that I might gain from defencing?"

"That would be unwise," said the professor, using the cane to point towards the Irishman's pocket. "You carry a cosh, whereas I am carrying a concealed pistol."

"Is this necessary?" I protested, interposing myself between the two men. The professor ignored my intrusion and continued to stare down the Irishman.

"Well, Mr Gahagan?"

Neither man's eyes gave anything away until Michael slowly withdrew his hand from his pocket and proffered it in a gesture of goodwill. Sensing the tension ease, I stepped aside.

"We have an understanding then, Mr Gahagan," Moriarty said, keeping his hands to himself. "You shall secure the service of men from two gangs—rivals would be best— and I shall reward you well for your loyalty. Dolly's Brae need never be mentioned again."

"Alright, I'll do it, but it'll cost you a pretty penny."

"I'm sure it will. Perhaps you would be so good as to see to the matter then. At your earliest convenience."

"Surely," said Michael, "but I'll be wanting to see the colour of your money first."

Moriarty's eyes narrowed, boring into Gahagan's soul for a moment. I

was filled with a sense of impending dread, which dissipated as the cold smile returned to his thin lips.

"Very well. I shall pay you on account in return for a small favour."

"What favour is that?"

Setting his stick aside once more, Moriarty indicated the far corner of the vault, and the second recessed arch there.

"Do you see the entrance?" He asked, indicating where two or three steps led up to a solid wooden door. "I want you to open it for me."

"Why me?"

"I have the key," said Moriarty, drawing a large and rather ornate old key from his pockets, "but I suspect it has been closed for about three hundred years. The priests within have little use for an entrance that leads into squalor."

"Priests?"

"Benedictine friars. Assuming they still use the place."

"What place, exactly?" Gahagan asked.

"I assumed that you were so well versed in the neighbourhood's secrets that you would already know where you are?"

"Aye," the Irishman confirmed, "this used to be part of the Rat's Castle, so it did."

"And before that?"

"Well, they found an old hospital in these parts a few years back."

"The leper's hospital, established by Queen Matilda, daughter of King Malcolm of Scotland. A devout Catholic. And do you know what this vault is?"

"No."

"Then let me enlighten you. That—" he indicated the wooden door "—is the rear entrance to the Chapel of St. John of Good Memory. Originally a private chapel, separate to St. Giles-in-the-Fields, where important visitors and senior priests would come to pray. It predates the hospital by three centuries, and its location has been closely guarded ever since the dissolution of the monasteries. Beyond that door lies a chamber filled with secrets."

"What sort of secrets?"

"Vatican secrets. All the documents with which the persecuted Catholics could escape, buried here and all but forgotten. There are as many valuables beyond that door as you will find in the Tower of London itself, Mr. Gahagan."

Was the professor provoking the Irishman? The Rats Castle had been a den of thieves. The Rookery was still a den of thieves. What better place to hide a treasure than under the noses of the city's villains? By association, that could only mean we, despite our respectable demeanour, were also being painted as thieves. Moriarty smiled.

"I can see the cogs turn, Mr. Gahagan. What would a professor and a priest be doing here? No less a Protestant priest in a Catholic vault?"

"I'll not rob the church..." Michael began.

"Indeed not. Nor would the reverend here allow it. As I said, I have the key."

Snatching the proffered object from the professor's hand, Gahagan waded across to the recess, and to the door at the top of the steps. There, he inserted the key and began to fight with the rusted old ward lock.

"Christ," he said, putting his shoulder to the door, "it's tough."

"We shall overcome, Mr Gahagan."

Minutes passed until, at last, the Irishman grunted and the door swung inwards.

"Excellent," said the professor. With a resigned sigh, he then drew the pistol from his pocket and discharged it into Gahagan's back.

I stood in amazement, frozen as I struggled to parse what I was seeing. My heart thumped in my chest and my skin tingled with shock and nausea. It all happened so... quickly. The sound of the gun had been curiously slight, but the payload had struck with such force that it pushed the Irishman to the wall, from whence he slid, sideways, into the water. It was the work of a moment, but it seemed to take forever, and the words were slow to tumble from my mouth.

"What in God's name...?"

"I apologize, reverend," said the professor, quite unapologetically. He placed a gloved hand on my arm, holding me back for a few more precious seconds. "I gave him the opportunity to leave, but his curiosity and greed seem to have got the better of him."

Brushing Moriarty aside, I dashed through the water to the side of the dying man. I was sick to the stomach and disoriented by the experience, my hands shaking as I lifted his head from the water.

"I realise that, as a man of God, you must abhor murder, reverend; this is certainly not my usual modus operandi, but... you know our plight. The end justifies the means."

"Nothing justifies murder!" I cried, still struggling to understand what had just happened. "You said he could be trusted."

"I lied to win his confidence. The man was loyal to a cause, but not to anything else. His cause is a Catholic Ireland, and any loyalty he had would be to those beyond the door. They would have heard his confession just as he heard ours. Gahagan was merely a low class thug whose life involved bullying and abusing others."

Sinking to my knees, I ignored

the stench of the brackish water and cradled Michael Gahagan, feeling his cooling breath against my tears. "How can you know this?"

"He was in my employ once before, when he was older and wiser. He still managed to shoot his mouth off and died with a bullet in the back, but on that occasion the finger on the trigger was not mine. Today, however, there was nobody to keep my hands clean. You might say that I have saved someone else's soul."

Looking up, I saw that the professor was now standing over us, reaching into his inside pocket.

"You cannot buy forgiveness from me!" I said, second guessing his intentions.

"Here..." he said, drawing out the slim pocketbook he had previously consulted. "It contains all the knowledge I have of the people in these parts, drawn from personal experience. I want you to read it— my past is laid bare, but it will help guide your thoughts."

"My thoughts? I don't understand," I was in shock. I was torn between a dying man and his murderer; between giving care and pacifying a cold hearted killer. "This man is going to die."

"And more will die. You stood beside me as I drew my pistol. You did not cry out a warning nor move to stop me. That is as it should be.

You need to be a witness. An observer. Stay by my side for as long as you can stomach it, and use the conscience I have abandoned in favour of science, logic and necessity.

"I need you to understand me like no other. Just as Sherlock Holmes will have his Doctor Watson, I must have a Boswell of my own. You must record our time together, and when the day of reckoning comes you shall use it as you see fit. History shall judge me in a way that neither the church nor the law can. Do you understand?"

I nodded dumbly. I did understand. I wished that I didn't but there, on my knees, the truth of my relationship with James Moriarty crystallized. With tears running down my cheeks, I delivered last rites as the light dimmed in Michael Gahagan's eyes.

***

"It is ironic," Moriarty had told me, "that the British Government could not trust their country's greatest detective with the case they brought to me. As an unparalleled broker of information, it was Mycroft Holmes who recommended me. Apparently his brother had too cosy a relationship with the Vatican to be approached by the most secret part of the Anglican Church. Answerable only to the Crown, the

Office of the Camera Stellata—the Star Chamber—has been one of the kingdom's best kept secrets since the abolition of the courts which it served in 1641."

As a minister myself, I had found it hard to believe the professor's story until he showed me the letter, bearing the Seal of the Palace of Whitehall, that warranted his investigation.

"I may not be a detective, but my network of agents within the criminal underworld was unsurpassed, and I was considered the only man outside the Vatican who might find and infiltrate the most important repository of forbidden texts beyond the Archivum Secretum. All they knew was that it lay somewhere within the St. Giles Rookery. I made my investigations, and quickly learned that the crows employed to protect the library were themselves in my employ. It was a simple matter to broker membership. Of course, some knowledge is too powerful to share, and so I reported my failure to the powers-that-be, but promised to keep an eye open should the library turn up."

I had been unfamiliar with the story of the Chapel of John of Good Memory until Moriarty had recounted it to me. John had not been a saint at all, but a devoted priest whose reputation as a pious scholar had earned him the epithet.

It had also earned him execution for heresy, and a second epithet—John the Beheaded. As a worshipper in the Church of St. John the Baptist in Devizes, the irony was not lost upon the founder of the leper's hospital, Queen Matilda, and so she named her private chapel after him, and subsequently had the contents of John's library transferred from St. Giles.

Unsanctioned by the Pope, it was John's custodianship of these books that led to his execution. The conflation of John with John the Baptist caused the Benedictines to take an interest and, when the Venetian Republic fell in 1797, the order was charged with indexing and protecting the site from the dreaded Church of England.

At first, the library had simply been an extensive collection of Gnostic and Christological texts from the earliest days of the church. Additional texts of a heretical, immoral or apostatic nature were soon added, and large swathes of correspondence and other discourses between the English Crown and the Sacred Court were added over the years. By the time King Henry VIII dissolved the monasteries, many early scientific and occult treatises had also come to be stored in the chapel. Finally, with the arrival of the Venetians, many of their own

precious books and works of art were added to the collection.

The professor had chosen not to wait for me as I laid Gahagan's body across our machine's cargo, after which I set foot into the 'chapel' alone, greeted by a black drape that rustled in a gentle breeze. Slipping past, I was surprised to find a dislodged wall of books—presumably Gahagan had toppled them when he forced the door—which led into a narrow, plushly carpeted corridor that was lined with rows of books and other documents piled twelve feet high, from floor to ceiling. They were illuminated—at ten foot intervals—by carefully-placed Davy lamps suspended from ceiling hooks. The corridor—which soon began to twist and turn like an ancient Greek labyrinth—did not feel like part of a chapel, and I surmised that the building comprised an entire level of the old hospital, spreading into its many rooms as its content expanded. The air, thick with dust and the unique smell of seven centuries' worth of hoarded parchment, vellum, and glue, was overwhelming as I pressed on, glancing into each small room that lined the way as I made slow progress towards the centre of the maze.

How much time I wasted time navigating through the labyrinthine structure I could not tell, but I eventually came to a large double door in the shape of an ogive arch. Finely carved from polished oak, it bore ornamental panels and the legend gloria in excelcis deo—Glory to God in the Highest—above its apex. This left me in no doubt that I was about the enter the chapel proper, and I took a careful grip on the medieval drop handles, pushing the doors open as respectfully as I could manage. The room beyond—unmistakably an old plain chapel—seemed incongruous, its bare white walls and lack of books drawing attention to the two objects which occupied the room. There was a plain wooden crucifix in the altar space, and there was a bare wooden desk at which a black monk sat, in the midst of a heated debate with the professor.

"Ah, reverend, you managed to catch up," said Moriarty, beckoning me over to meet the priest. "This is Brother Arminius, the curator and head librarian, formerly of the Order of Saint Benedict."

"Formerly?" I asked, nodding towards the friar.

"Yes, you missed the negotiations I'm afraid. We have come to an arrangement. Brother Arminius and Brother Ambrosius—who is currently indisposed—feel that preserving the secrecy of the library and its contents is of greater

importance than their holy orders. I shall be making this place our base of operations for the forseeable future. In return for my patronage they shall continue to perform their duties as if they remained in service to the Bishop of Rome."

This shock revelation seemed an impossibility to me, even for someone as wily as Moriarty. I could see that the priest was both red faced and wide-eyed—a sure sign that he had been afraid for his life—certainly enough to offer no challenge to the professor's announcement. Taking Moriarty by the elbow, I excused us from the friar and drew him aside.

"What is this? Priests don't just give up their beliefs in polite debate. What did you do?"

"There are certain crimes, reverend, that the laws of England will not excuse, no matter how carefully the Catholic church might attempt to cover them up. There is a certain house of ill-repute situated two minutes' walk from the Strand, where children are forced against their will to... pay lip service to their elders. These brothers have recently been celebrating matins and vespers at that house on a very regular basis. They would have continued to do so for a further twenty years."

My heart froze at this appalling revelation, which left me in a worse state than even the killing of Michael Gahagan. As before, Moriarty drew documents from his coat pocket and pressed them into my hands.

"I have presented them with this evidence of their crimes and secured their promise that they shall never set foot outside this library again, and that no child shall ever enter. I shall find other roughs to take Gahagan's place as my agents here, and they will preserve the arrangement. In return for my silence, the brothers have agreed to report the destruction of the library by fire in a desperate attempt to prevent it from falling into the hands of the Star Chamber."

I resisted the urge to demand the professor's pistol to exact revenge of my own, but my personal faith held. Through gritted teeth and clenched fists I controlled my anger, turning back towards the friar, whose expression confirmed everything at the moment our eyes met. Unable to hold my gaze, he looked away in shame and I, a moment later, did the same, casting my eyes downwards where I spied a single drop of blood on the paving stones. Did I want to know what befell the other priest? Could he be dead at Moriarty's hand?

"I need the librarians, reverend," said the professor—as if reading my mind and offering some degree of reassurance, "at least until their replacements can be trained. Brother Ambrosius will live."

***

And so we took up lodgings in the Rookery, at least for a time. Moriarty was true to his word, recruiting a couple of local gangs to police the library on his behalf. He had a way of dealing with the criminal classes that I could almost admire—it was as if they saw him as their natural superior in matters of intellect, deferring to the calm logic of his arguments without question. I saw no repeat of the incident with Gahagan, and while he assured me he had no intention of building a second criminal empire, it seemed clear to me that it might still exist as a natural consequence of such interactions.

In a matter of weeks the chapel was again secure, its criminal bodyguards were put in place, and the precious cargo that lay at the heart of our plans—a large quantity of gold bullion to be minted into sovereigns by the local coiners, and a large quantity of printed material to be distributed to those that Moriarty wished to court—had been unloaded.

We then used Moriarty's time machine to give Michael Gahagan the burial I had insisted upon. Arriving in darkness during the winter months of 1106, I chose to bury the body in a shallow ditch that ran alongside the old Saxon chapel where John of Good Memory had been chaplain. The ground was hard, but I insisted on performing the labour alone. The professor stood respectfully—or, I could but hope, shamefully—some distance away as I performed the nocturnal service, leaving his victim beneath a simple headstone that gave no clue that he was a man from the future. I wondered, as we returned to our new lodgings, just how many more bodies might be buried here by my hand.

THE STEAMPUNK CANON

by Adrian Middleton

The rather ambitious aim of The Moriarty Paradigm is to create an alternative canon of steampunk adventures starring Sherlock Holmes and Doctor Watson. As a popular subject for steampunk adventures, the idea that writers need to create their own entirely original steampunk universes just to tell such stories, seems quite overwhelming. Instead we thought, over a glass of half-and-half and a pipeful of shag, that we might try and create a consistent world whose rules are fixed enough to allow consistency between the many mash-ups and original steampunk tales that Holmes might occupy.

To achieve this, our interpretation of the original Sherlock Holmes canon (which we call The Holmes Paradigm) needs, at the very least, to be consistent. With so many varied interpretations of the canon, it would be easy for stories to deviate from a set of agreed facts. For this reason, our starting point is to establish the basics, in much the same way that William S Baring Gould (in Sherlock Holmes of Baker Street: A life of the world's first consulting detective), Vincent Starrett (in The Private Life of Sherlock Holmes),

Nick Rennison (in Sherlock Holmes: The Unauthorized Biography) and many others have attempted to do.

Our approach has been three fold.

In the first instance, we have the opportunity—by editing Doyle's original stories to address contradictions, inconsistencies and loopholes—to create a reliable continuity in much the same way as would be seen in a modern publication or production. Even before applying this to mash-ups and new stories, we have applied it to character notes and to the guidelines we provide our writers.

In the second instance, we have been able to review the many arguments and counter arguments relating to continuity within the original Holmes canon, applying those arguments we feel to be most consistent, adopting a timeline and order of stories which best fit the story we want to tell. To support this timeline, we intend to publish these stories—where possible—in chronological order.

Finally, we have examined the many apocryphal facts attributed to the history of Holmes and Watson by various experts. Many of these

'facts' have been adopted by writers and incorporated into new and original fiction involving the great detective. Following in this tradition, we have ourselves chosen to adopt some of the background that many have come, erroneously, to believe.

I. Character Notes

The key recurring characters that appear in The Moriarty Paradigm, while differing slightly from their canonical counterparts, are essentially the same characters Doyle created. While the only variations we see are those that occur as direct result of changes to historical events, those details influenced by our interpretation of the original Doyle stories are presented here:

Billy the Page: Billy is a staple supporting character throughout Holmes' career, having an active role between 1887 and 1900. We assume that Sherlock Holmes rescued Billy from the local workhouse, at the age of ten, at Christmas in 1887, and has paid for his lodgings at 221b Baker Street to assist Mrs Hudson in her role as landlady. This guarantees Holmes a greater degree of service that the other inhabitants of the Baker Street apartments. During his tenure with Mrs Hudson, Billy works from six in the morning until ten at night.

Mycroft Holmes: The relationship between Mycroft and Sherlock, while both affable and competitive on the surface, is strained by recent family events. Their careers have been enabled by the existence of an older brother—Sherrinford—who took over the family's Wetherby estates from their father until his death in 1887. As the older of the remaining siblings, Mycroft has family duties that he appears to resent. Their relationship is further compromised by the activities of Professor Moriarty, who is known to Mycroft and who takes a much more political role as the stories develop.

As far as Mycroft's day job is concerned, it remains ambiguous at the offset, just as it is in the original canon. As described by Doyle, "occasionally he is the British government . . . the most indispensable man in the country".

Sherlock Holmes: Most of Holmes' background remains unchanged. He spent only two years at University, leaving early and failing to graduate. He then spent a year as a consulting detective before he took up lodgings in Montague Street, where he remained for nearly five years prior to moving into Baker Street. His companion prior to Dr Watson was an engineer called Ormond Sacker, about whom Holmes is reluctant to speak.

Sherrinford Holmes: Like his father, Sherrinford Holmes never appeared in the original canon, being a creation of William S. Baring Gould. Sherrinford was born in India during his father's service with the British East India Company, and was the eldest of three brothers, inheriting the family estate near Wetherby in Yorkshire and managing it until his death in 1887. The circumstances of this death are currently unknown.

Siger Holmes: The father of the Holmes brothers Siger is, like his eldest son Sherrinford, a Baring-Gould creation who never appeared in Doyle's fiction. We know that he served as an officer in the British East India Company between 1843 and 1853, returning to India some years later where he died in 1873.

Mrs Hudson: Holmes' landlady remains faithful to the original. She is a widow whose primary income comes from the apartments that she rents out to Holmes and other tenants. In the early years, before 1887, she has other staff who, one by one, she lets go. The change in Holmes' fortunes as a result of his success leads to the appointment of the page boy Billy, and in subsequent years she develops an almost maternal fondness for the boy.

Brigadier Bastion Moran: Moran's fortunes are significantly altered by changes in history. Our version of Moran avoids scandal when, in 1856, his father is appointed as Lieutenant-Governor of India. While his nature is unchanged, he is promoted to command the First Air Rifles, the British Army's company of dedicated aerial sharpshooters. The consequences of these changes remain to be seen.

James Moriarty: Professor Moriarty is the character around which our steampunk universe revolves—the spider at the heart of the web that is the British Empire. In this world he is an influential politician, a highly successful philanthropist and a committed atheist with lofty and inscrutable goals that will bring him to the attention of Sherlock Holmes.

Mary Morstan: Following an annulled marriage in early 1888, John Watson became entangled in the affairs of Miss Mary Morstan, and a romance developed. They are married before the year is out, and their fate is in our hands.

Arthur Murray: Murray was serving as a Medical Orderly with the Berkshires when his personal bravery saved the life of John Watson at the Battle of Maiwand. A cockney,

Murray remained in Afghanistan, transferring to the New East India Company until his eventual return to England.

Ormond Sacker: Before John Watson there was Ormond Sacker. Recorded as a name that Doyle considered for his great detective, we have chosen to realise sacker as an insight into Holmes' early years. As an American of Scottish ancestry, our version of Sacker was an engineering graduate acquainted with Holmes at university, and went on to share lodgings with him for three or four years at Montague Street, where the two men developed a similar relationship to that enjoyed by Holmes and Watson.

One or two years prior to Holmes' meeting with Watson, Ormond Sacker disappeared under mysterious circumstances during a case that Holmes never mentions. Through Sacker's own accounts we learn that he shared Holmes' interest in criminal investigation, and that they worked together, but more often as rivals than as partners. As an engineer Sacker was a champion of inductive reasoning, a method that conflicts with Holmes deductive approach.

The Stamfords: 'Young Stamford' is the only mutual friend of Holmes and Watson, and is a medical man who works at St. Barts Hospital between 1881 and 1888, after which he and Watson set up a medical practice in Farringdon. Their friendship forms a contract to that of Holmes and Watson, but becomes strained following an unhappy dalliance between Watson and Stamford's sister.

Encouraged by Stamford, Watson became involved with his sister, whom he eventually married in early 1888. This was a short and quickly curtailed affair that lasted only three months as she required that her husband sever all ties with Holmes. Claiming not to have consummated the marriage, its annulment forced Watson to abandon his share in the Farringdon practice, leading to severe financial hardship until Stamford, from whom he was estranged, could repay him.

Nikola Tesla: Tesla's life is transformed when, in 1873, his Serbian maths tutor—Martin Sekulić—arranges for his sponsorship and transfer to St John's College, Cambridge, where he trains as an engineer. Unaware that this has spared him military service and exposure to tuberculosis, Nikola quickly adapts to life in England and, in 1879, becomes a major shareholder in Westinghouse Electric.

Victor Trevor: Victor was Sherlock Holmes' only real friend at university, and was in part responsible for turning Holmes towards his life as a detective. He is a dog lover, having owned at least one bull terrier (something he has in common with Watson).

John Watson: As a military doctor, Watson trained as a surgeon at Netley Hospital, and was shipped out to serve aboard the aerostat Keane in 1878. The Keane was a relief aerostat assigned to give medical aid to British Troops during the Second Afghan War. After 20 months of service, Watson was injured over Maiwand when Afghan rebels succeeded in shooting down the Keane, which erupted into flames and crashed in the mountains over the Panjshir Valley. As the senior surviving officer, Watson— with the assistance of his orderly Arthur Murray—led his men home through hostile territory to safety and was mentioned in despatches.

Throughout his life with Holmes, John Watson leads a second life. He practices medicine with Stamford at St. Barts, and later participates in at least three different medical practices—Farringdon (with Stamford in early 1888), Paddington (purchased from Dr. Farquhar in late 1888-1891), and Kensington (from 1891).

As the narrator of Holmes' adventures, Watson's published stories withheld much information about his own character, playing down his personal heroism and the ease with which he finds himself manipulated by women. He treads a fine line between respecting woman and being seen as a womaniser, and this ambiguity makes it hard for him to hold down a relationship for very long. Our storied are presented as unedited accounts, where aspects of Watson's personal life are more visible, and where his insights into Holmes' personal life are unredacted.

Wiggins and the Baker Street Irregulars: Recruited as required for a shilling a day plus expenses, the Irregulars, numbering between six and a dozen boys at any time, were originally "street Arabs".

Wiggins leads the Irregulars from 1887 until some time after 1890, when he will be replaced by a boy called Simpson some time before 1893.

2. TIMELINE

We can't reveal all of our alternative steampunk timeline, as that would perhaps give away some of the events to come. The overarching history of the British Empire will change, diverging more and more as

time passes. Watson's diaries begin on Tuesday, 20th March 1888, and Holmes' adventures will be told in chronological order from that date forwards. Stories set during Holmes' early years (prior to 1888) will be recounted by Watson as flashbacks when most appropriate.

Events prior to 1856 are identical in the original Holmes timeline (The Holmes Paradigm) and in the alternative steampunk timeline we are recounting here (The Moriarty Paradigm). How and why will be revealed in forthcoming stories. Key events are as follows:

1800: Baron Franz Xavier von Zach establishes the Lilenthal Society in Bremen. Later known as the Himmelspolizei ("Celestial Police"), this group attempted to discover a planet located between Mars and Jupiter. Instead they and their contemporaries began to discover the asteroid belt.

1815: The Himmelspolizei disband. Many of their papers will end up in the hands of Professor James Moriarty, who is born 19 years later, in 1834.

1843-1853: Siger Holmes serves as an officer of the British East India Company. His eldest son, Sherrinford, is born at this time.

1852: John H. Watson is born.

1854: Sherlock Holmes is born.

1855: James Moriarty completes a Treatise on the Binomial Theorem.

After 1856 the two histories diverge, although the lives of Holmes and Watson remain consistent, with little deviation between the original Holmes world and the steampunk one. Key events leading up to the first published Holmes adventure are as follows:

1856-60: James Moriarty establishes a reputation as a speculator and shrewd financier, investing in a wide range of new, experimental technologies. He is soon appointed to the East India Company's Court of Directors.

1857: The sepoys of the East India Company rebel against the British and are defeated at the hands of the first British Army Aerostat Company. Sir Augustus Moran is appointed as a Lieutenant Governor of India.

1858: James Moriarty publicly supports four major projects:
• Joseph Bazalgette and London's Metropolitan Board of Works' plans to tackle the Great Stink;

- Charles Pearson's proposals to the City of London Corporation for a subterranean railway;
- Aimé Thomé de Gamond's proposals to Napoleon III for a Channel Tunnel;
- The East Africa Company's expedition to survey Mount Kilima-Njaro.

1862: The first commercial steam-powered airship company, established by James Moriarty, creates a transport revolution. Railway and canal companies force legislation to secure themselves a share of the new industry.

1866: The Panic of 1866 causes an international financial downturn. James Moriarty emerges richer and more successful, becoming the principal investor in Britain's transport infrastructure.

1872: Sherlock Holmes goes to Oxford, where he fails to graduate.

1872-1878: Springheeled Jack or The Rossian Bear terrorizes Peckham and other parts of London.

1873: While Siger Holmes dies in India, Mount Kilima-Njaro becomes the base for an Industrial-scale space-cannon sending supplies to the moon in advance of a lunar landing.

1874: The first manned capsule is fired into space by the Mount Kilima-Njaro space cannon.

1875: A British Lunar Expeditionary Force claims and begins colonising the moon. Germany and America announce similar programmes to put colonies on the moon.

1877-1880: Sherlock Holmes shares rooms with a man called Ormond Sacker in Montague Street, where he embarks upon his first cases as a consulting detective.

1878: Holmes and Sacker notably solve The Case of Spring-Heeled Jack's Return.

1879: Watson goes to Afghanistan.

1880-1890: Indoor gas lamps start to be replaced with electric incandescent lamps.

1880: John Watson is injured when a relief aerostat is shot down during the Battle of Maiwand in the second Afghan War. This leaves him with an injured left hand side and a fear of flying. In England, James Moriarty becomes the Conservative Member of Parliament for Cambridge University and invests in pneumatic mining.

1881: John Watson meets Sherlock Holmes. Meanwhile, work on the Channel Tunnel commences and is completed within a year. The tunnel uses a pneumatic system, and includes the fixing of mooring masts for a tethered aerostat transit system.

1882: The first successful war waged by an aerial fleet secures Egypt under British rule. In the same the Bell Teslaphone is introduced and The Electric Power Bill brings safe broadcast power to Britain.

1883: The East Africa Company uses pneumatic pressure to bring water from the Mediterranean and the Red Sea to create permanent rain clouds over the Sahara.

1884: A Treaty between the major powers sees Britain share the Moon with other nations. France, Germany and the United States begin a race to colonize the moon.

1887: The death of Sherrinford Holmes creates tension between his younger brothers, Sherlock and Mycroft.

3. Ex–Canon Apocrypha

A number of Holmes scholars (most notably William S. Baring-Gould and Vincent Starrett)

have made assumptions about certain facts within the Sherlock Holmes canon which have been adopted in subsequent Holmes apocrypha. To preserve consistency within the series, our take on these assumptions are as follows:

Did Holmes travel through Europe as a child, and later tour America as an actor? No. The books were clear that Holmes spent some time consulting. We assume he did this with Ormond Sacker, who was an American, and who disappeared before Watson came on the scene. Having an American as a close acquaintance gives Holmes some insight into life on the other side of the Atlantic.

Was Moriarty Holmes' mathematics tutor? No. Moriarty ends up as the Chair of Mathematics at a lesser Cambridge College, while Holmes attended Oxford.

Did Sherlock and Mycroft have an older brother, Sherrinford, who manages the family's estates? Yes. The idea of an older brother adds a layer of background we can use.

Did Watson's early years include a trip to San Francisco, where he married Constance Adams, his first wife? Not quite. We're following Conan Doyle's play The Angel of

Darkness, in which Watson was present during the flashback part of A Study in Scarlet, and ended up engaged to Lucy Ferrier. There is no assumption, however, that they got married.

Was Holmes closely connected to Jack the Ripper? Who knows? Best to leave this open to be addressed later.

Was Mycroft the head of British intelligence? He is high up, but his exact position stays unclear – he is the clearing house, the majordomo behind the scene. He isn't necessarily the boss, but he is the one through whom all information flows.

Did Holmes use 'royal jelly' to maintain his youthful vigour and live to a great age, dying in 1939 or 1957? Who knows? Who cares? Right now we don't even know if he'll be surviving The Final Problem.

Was Holmes born January 6, 1854, at 'Mycroft' in the North Riding of Yorkshire? We agree that he was born in 1854 but the date isn't to be revealed. We place the estate, unnamed, nearer to Wetherby, also in Yorkshire.

Does The Hound of the Baskervilles overlap with the Jack the Ripper murders? No.

Did Watson marry three times? He certainly marries twice. What happens with Mary Morstan is open to question.

Did Holmes have an affair with Irene Adler in 1892? Unlikely, Watson is our preferred womaniser.

Was Mrs Hudson Holmes' housekeeper? No, she was his landlady. She may well retire to become Holmes' housekeeper in Sussex, but that's a story for another day.

A VISIT TO THE ROOKERY OF ST. GILES AND ITS NEIGHBOURHOOD

by Henry Mayhew

The following essay, extracted from the pages of Henry Mayhew's London Labour and the London Poor (published between 1841 and 1861) serves as an introduction to a part of London that plays a key role in The Moriarty Paradigm series. Just as Holmes has 221b Baker Street and Mycroft has the Diogenes Club, our Moriarty also has a base of operations: The chapel of St. John of Good Memory:

In company with a police officer we proceeded to the Seven Dials, one of the most remarkable localities in London, inhabited by bird-fanciers, keepers of old stores of old clothes and old shoes, costermongers, patterers, and a motley assemblage of others, chiefly of the lower classes. As we stood at one of the angles in the centre of the Dials we saw three young men—burglars—loitering at an opposite corner of an adjoining dial. One of them had a gentlemanly appearance, and was dressed in superfine black cloth and beaver hat. The other two were attired as mechanics or tradesmen. One of them had recently returned from penal servitude, and another had undergone a long imprisonment.

Leaving the Seven Dials and its dingy neighbourhood, we went to Oxford Street, one of the first commercial streets in London, and one of the finest in the world. It reminded us a good deal of the celebrated Broadway, New York, although the buildings of the latter are in some places more costly and splendid, and some of the shops more magnificent. Oxford Street is one of the main streets of London, and is ever resounding with the din of vehicles, carts, cabs, hansoms, broughams, and omnibuses driving along. Many of the shops are spacious and crowded with costly goods, and the large windows of pate-glass, set in massive brass frames, are gaily furnished with their various articles of merchandise.

On the opposite side of the street we observed a jolly, comfortable-looking, elderly man, like a farmer in appearance, not at all like a London sharper. He was standing looking along the street as though he were waiting for some one. He was a

magsman (a skittle-sharp), and no doubt other members of the gang were hovering near. He appeared to be as cunning as an old fox in his movements, admirably fitted to entrap the unwary.

A little farther along the street we saw a fashionably-dressed man coming towards us, arm in arm with his companion, among the throng of people. They were in the prime of life, and had a respectable, and even opulent appearance. One of them was good-humoured and social, as though he were on good terms with himself and society in general; the other was more callous and reserved, and more suspicious in his aspect. Both were bedecked with glittering watch-chains and gold rings. They passed by a few paces, when the more social of the two, looking over his shoulder, met our eye directed towards him, turned back and accosted us, and was even so generous as to invite us into a gin-palace near by, which we courteously declined. The two magsmen (card-sharpers) strutted off, like fine gentlemen, along the street on the outlook for their victims.

Here we saw another young man, a burglar, pass by. He had an engaging appearance, and was very tasteful in his dress, very unlike the rough burglars we met at Whitechapel, the Borough, and Lambeth.

Leaving Oxford Street we went along Holborn to Chancery Lane, chiefly frequented by barristers and attorneys, and entered Fleet Street, one of the main arteries of the metropolis, reminding us of London in the olden feudal times, when the streets were crowded together in dense masses, flanked with innumerable dingy alleys, courts, and by-streets, like a great rabbit-warren. Fleet Street, though a narrow, business street, with its traffic often choked with vehicles, is interesting from its antique, historical, and literary associations. Elbowing our way through the throng of people, we pass through one of the gloomy arches of Temple Bar, and issue into the Strand, where we saw two pickpockets, young, tall, gentlemanly men, cross the street from St. Clement's Church and enter a restaurant. They were attired in a suit of superfine black cloth, cut in fashionable style. They entered an elegant dining-room, and probably sat down to costly viands and wines.

Leaving the Strand, we went up St. Martin's Lane, a narrow street leading from the Strand to the Seven Dials. We here saw a young man, an expert burglar, of about twenty-four years of age and dark complexion, standing at the corner of the street. He was well dressed, in a dark cloth suit, with a billicock hat. One of his

comrades was taken from his side about three weeks ago on a charge of burglary.

Entering a beershop in the neighbourhood of St. Giles, close by the Seven Dials, we saw a band of coiners and ringers of changes. One of them, an genteel-looking, slim youth is a notorious coiner, and has been convicted. He was sitting quietly by the door over a glass of beer, with his companion by his side. One of them is a moulder; another was sentenced to ten years' penal servitude for coining and selling base coin. A modest-looking young man, one of the gang, was seated by the bar, also respectably dressed. He is generally supposed to be a subordinate connected with this coining band, looking out, while they are coining, that no officers of justice are near, and carrying the bag of base money for them when they go out to sell it to base wretches in small quantities at low prices. Five shillings' worth of base money is generally sold for ten pence. Ringing the changes is effected in this way:—A person offers a good sovereign to a shopkeeper to be changed. The gold piece is chinked on the counter, or otherwise tested, ad is proved to be good. The man hastily asks back and gets the sovereign, and pretends that he has some silver, so that he does not require to change it. On feeling his pocket he does not have it, and returns a base piece of money resembling it, instead of the genuine gold piece.

We returned to Bow Street, and saw three young pickpockets proceeding along in company, like three well-dressed costermongers, in dark cloth frock-coats and caps.

Being desirous of having a more thorough knowledge of the people in the rookery of St. Giles, we visited it with Mr. Hunt, inspector of police. We first went to a lodging-house in George Street, Oxford Street, called the Hampshire Hog Yard. Most of the lodgers were then out. On visiting a room in the garret we saw a man, in mature years, making artificial flowers; he appeared to be very ingenious, and made several roses before us with marvellous rapidity. He had suspended along the ceiling bundles of dyed grasses of various hues, crimson, yellow, green, brown, and other colours to furnish cases of stuffed birds. He was a very intelligent man and a natural genius. He told us that strong drink had brought him to this humble position in the garret, and that he once had the opportunity of making a fortune in the service of a nobleman. We felt, as we looked on his countenance, an listened to his conversation, he was capable of moving in a higher sphere of life. Et

he was wonderfully contented with his humble lot.

We visited Dyott House, George Street, the ancient manor-house of St. Giles-in-the-Fields, now fitted up as a lodging-house for single men. The kitchen, an apartment about fifteen feet square, is surrounded with massive and tasteful panelling in the olden style. A large fire blazing in the grate—with two boilers on each side—was kept burning night and day to supply the lodgers with hot water for their tea and coffee. Some rashers of bacon were suspended before the fire, with a plate underneath. There was a gas-light in the centre of the apartment, and a dial on the back wall. The kitchen was furnished with two long deal tables and a dresser, with forms to serve as seats. There were about fifteen labouring men present, most of them busy at supper on fish, and bread, and tea. They were a very mixed company, such as we would expect at a London lodging-house, men working in cab-yards assisting cabmen, some distributing bills in the streets, one man carrying advertising boards, and others jobbing at anything they can find to do in the neighbourhood. The house was clean and comfortable and had the appearance of being truly a comfortable poor man's home. It was cheerful to look around us and to see the social air of the inmates. One man sat with his coat off, enjoying the warmth of the kitchen; a boy was at his tea, cutting up dried fish and discussing his bread and butter. A young man of about nineteen sat at the back of the apartment, with a very sinister countenance, very unlike the others. There was something about him that indicated a troubled mind. We also observed a number of elderly men among the party, some in jackets and others in velvet coats, with an honest look about them.

When the house was a brothel, about fifteen years ago, an unfortunate prostitute, named Mary Brothers, was murdered in this kitchen by a man named Connell, who was afterwards executed at Newgate for the deed. He had carnal connexion with this woman some time before, and he suspected that she had communicated to him the venereal disease with which he was afflicted. In revenge he took her life, having purchased a knife at the neighbouring cutler's shop.

We were introduced to the landlady, a very stout woman, who came up to meet us, candle in hand, as we stood on the staircase. Here we saw the profile of the ancient proprietor of the house, carved over the panelling, set, as it were, in an oval frame. In another part of the staircase we saw a similar frame, but the profile had been removed or destroyed. Over the window that overlooks the staircase there are three figures, possibly likenesses of his daughters; such is the tradition. The balustrade along the staircase is very massive and tastefully carved and ornamented. The bedrooms were also clean and comfortable.

The beds are furnished with a bed-cover and flock-bed, with sufficient warm and clean bedding, for the low charge of 2s. a week, or 4d.a night. The first proprietor of the house is said to have been a magistrate of the city, and a knight or baronet.

Leaving George Street we passed on to Church Lane, a by-street in the rear of New Oxford Street, containing twenty-eight houses. It was dark as we passed along. We saw the street-lamps lighted in Oxford Street, and the shop-windows brilliantly illumined, while the thunder of vehicles in the street broke on our ear, rolling in perpetual stream. Here a very curious scene presented itself to our view. From the windows of the three-storied houses in Church Lane were suspended wooden rods with clothes to dry across the narrow street,—cotton gowns, sheets, trousers, drawers, and vests, some ragged and patched, and others old and faded, giving a more picturesque aspect to the scene, which was enhanced by the dim lights in the windows, and the groups of the lower orders of all ages assembled below, clustered around the doorways, and in front of the houses, or indulging in merriment in the street. Altogether the appearance of the inhabitants was much more clean and orderly than might be expected in such a low locality. Many women of the lower orders, chiefly of the Irish cockneys, were seated, crouching with their knees almost touching their chin, beside the open windows. Some men were smoking their pipes as they stood leaning against the walls of their houses whom from their appearance we took to be evidently outdoor labourers. Another labouring man was seated on the sill of his window, in corduroy trousers, light-grey coat and cap, with an honest look of good humour and industry. Numbers of young women, the wives of costermongers, sat in front of their houses in the manner we have described, clad in cotton gowns, with a general aspect of personal cleanliness and contentment. At the corners of the streets, and at many of the doorways, were groups of young costermongers, who had finished their days' hard work, and were contentedly chatting and smoking. They generally stood with their hands in their breeches pockets. Most of these people are

Irish, or the children of Irish parents. The darkness of the street was lighted up by the street lamps as well as by the lights in the windows of two chandlers' shops and one public house. At one of the chandlers' shops the proprietor was standing by his door with folded arms as he looked good-humouredly on his neighbours around his shop-door. We also saw some of the young Arabs bareheaded and barefooted, with their little hands in their pockets, or squatted on the street, having the usual restless, artful look peculiar to their tribe.

Here a house was pointed out to us, No. 21, which was formerly let at a rent of £25 per annum to a publican that resided in the neighbourhood. He let the same rooms for £90 a year, and these again receive from parties residing in them upwards of £120. The house is still let in rooms, but they are occupied, like all the others in the neighbourhood, by one family only.

At one house as we passed along we saw a woman selling potatoes, at the window, to persons in the street. On looking into the interior we saw a cheerful fire burning in the grate and some women sitting around it. We also observed several bushel baskets and sacks placed round the room, filled with potatoes, of which they sell a large quantity.

In Church Lane we found two lodging-houses, the kitchens of which are entered from the street by a descent of a few steps leading underground to the basement. Here we found numbers of people clustered together around several tables, some reading the newspapers, others supping on fish, bread, tea, and potatoes, and some lying half asleep on the tables in all imaginable positions. These, we were told, had just returned from hopping in Kent, had walked long distances, and were fatigued.

On entering some of these kitchens, the ceiling being very low, we found a large fire burning in the grate, and a general air of comfort, cleanliness, and order. Such scenes as these were very homely and picturesque, and reminded us very forcibly of localities in London in the olden time. In some of them the inmates were only half dressed, ad yet appeared to be very comfortable from the warmth of the apartment. Here we saw a number of the poorest imbeciles we had noticed in the course of our rambles through the great metropolis. Many of them were middle-aged men, others more elderly, very shabbily dressed, and some half naked. There was little manliness left in the poor wretches as they squatted drearily on the benches. The inspector told us they were chiefly vagrants, and were sunk in profound ignorance and

debasement, from which they were utterly unable to rise.

The next kitchen of this description we entered was occupied by females. It was about fifteen feet square, and belongs to a house with ten rooms, part of which is occupied as a low lodging-house. Here we found five women seated around a table, most of them young, but one more advanced in life. Some of them were good-looking, as though they had been respectable servants. They were busy at their tea, bread, and butcher's meat. On the table stood a candle on a small candlestick. They sat in curious positions around the table, some of them with an ample crinoline. One sat by the fire with her gown drawn over her knees, displaying her white petticoat. As we stood beside them they burst out in a titter which they could not suppress. On looking round we observed a plate-rack a the back of the kitchen, and, as usual in these lodging-houses, a glorious fire burning brightly in the grate. An old chest of drawers, surmounted with shelves, stood against the wall. The girls were all prostitutes and thieves, but had no appearance of shame. They were apparently very merry. The old woman sat very thoughtful, looking observant on, and no doubt wondering what errand could have brought us into the house.

We then entered another dwelling-house. On looking down the stairs we saw a company of young women, from seventeen to twenty-five years of age. A rope was hung over the fireplace, with stockings and shirts suspended over it, and clothes were drying on a screen. A young woman, with her hair netted and ornamented, sat beside the fire with a green jacket and striped petticoat with crinoline. Another good-looking young woman sat by the table dressed in a cotton gown and striped apron, with coffee-pot in hand, and tea-cups before her. Some pleasant-looking girls sat by the table with their chins leaning on their hands, smiling cheerfully, looking at us with curiosity. Another coarser featured dame lolled by the end of the table with her gown drawn over her head, smirking in our countenance; and one sat by, her shawl drawn over her head. Another apparently modest girl sat by cutting her nails with a knife. On the walls around the apartment were suspended a goodly assortment of bonnets, cloaks, gowns and petticoats.

Meantime an elderly little man came in with a cap on his head and a long staff in his hand, and stood looking on with curiosity. On the table lay a pack of cards beside the bowls, cups, and other crockery-ware. Some of the girls appeared as if they had lately been servants in

respectable situations, and one was like a quiet genteel shop-girl. They were all prostitutes, and most of them prowl about at night to plunder drunken men. As we looked on the more interesting girls, especially two of them, we saw the sad consequences of one wrong step, which may launch the young and thoughtless into a criminal career, and drive them into the dismal companionship of the most lewd and debased.

We then went to Short's Gardens, and entered a house there. On the basement underground we saw a company of men, women, and children of various ages, seated around the tables, and by the fire. The men and women had mostly been engaged in hopping, and appeared to be healthy, industrious, and orderly. Until lately thieves used to lodge in these premises.

As we entered Queen Street we saw three thieves, lads of about fourteen years of age, standing in the middle of the street as if on the outlook for booty. They were dressed in black frock-coats, corduroy, and fustian trousers, and black caps. Passing along Queen Street, which is one of the wings of the Dials, we went up to the central space between the Seven Dials. Here a very lively scene presented itself to our view; clusters of labouring men, and a few men of doubtful character, in dark shabby dress, loitered by the corners of the surrounding streets. We also saw groups of elderly women standing at some of the angles, most of them ragged and drunken, their very countenances the pictures of abject misery. The numerous public houses in the locality were driving a busy traffic, and were thronged with motley groups of people of various grades, from the respectable merchant and tradesman to the thief and the beggar.

Bands of boys and girls were gambolling in the street in wild frolic, tumbling on their head with their heels in the air, and shouting in merriment, while the policeman was quietly looking on in god humour.

Around the centre of the Dials were bakers' shops with large illuminated fronts, the shelves being covered with loaves, and the baker busy attending to his customers. In the window was a large printed notice advertising the "best wheaten bread at 6d." a loaf. A druggist's shop was invitingly adorned with beautiful green and purple jars, but no customers entered during the time of our stay.

At the corner of an opposite dial was an old clothes store, with a large assortment of second-hand garments, chiefly for men, of various kinds, qualities, and styles, suspended around the front of the shop. There were also provision shops, which were

well attended with customers. The whole neighbourhood presented an appearance of bustle and animation, and omnibuses and other vehicles were passing along in a perpetual stream.

The most of the low girls in this locality do not go out till late in the evening, and chiefly devote their attention to drunken men. They frequent the principal thoroughfares in the vicinity of Oxford Street, Holborn, Farringdon Street, and other bustling streets. From the nature of their work they are of a migratory character. The most of the men we saw in the houses we visited belong to the labouring class, men employed to assist in cleaning cabs and omnibuses, carriers of advertising boards, distributors of bills, patterers, chickweed sellers, ballad singers, and persons generally of industrious habits, along with a few of doubtful character. They are willing to work, but will steal rather than want.

The lodging-house people here have not been known of late years to receive stolen property, and the inhabitants generally are steadily rising in habits of decency, cleanliness, and morality.

The houses we visited in George Street, and the streets adjacent, were formerly part of the rookery of St. Giles-in-the-Fields, celebrated as one of the chief haunts of redoubtable thieves and suspicious characters in London. Deserted as it comparatively is now, except by the labouring poor vagrants and low prostitutes, it was once the resort of all classes, from the proud noble to the beggar picking up a livelihood from door to door.

We have been indebted to Mr. Hunt, inspector of the lodging-houses of this district, for fuller information regarding the rookery of St. Giles and its inhabitants twenty years ago, before a number of these disreputable streets were removed to make way for New Oxford Street. We quote from a manuscript nearly in his own words:—

"The ground covered by the Rookery was enclosed by Great Russell Street, Charlotte Street, Broad Street, and High Street, all within the parish of St. Giles-in-the-Fields. Within this space were George Street (once Dyott Street), Carrier Street, Maynard Street, and Church Street, which ran from north to south, and were intersected by Church Lane, Ivy Lane, Buckeridge Street, Bainbridge Street, and New Street. These, within an almost endless intricacy of courts and yards crossing each other, rendered the place like a rabbit-warren.

"In Buckeridge Street stood the Hare and Hounds public house,

formerly the Beggar in the Bush; at the time of which I speak (1844) kept by the well-known and much-respected Joseph Banks (generally called 'Stunning Joe'), a civil, rough, good-hearted Boniface. His house was the resort of all classes, from the aristocratic marquis to the vagabond whose way of living was a puzzle to himself.

"At the opposite corner of Carrier Street stood Mother Dowling's, a lodging-house and provision shop, which was not closed nor the shutters put on for several years before it was pulled down, to make way for the improvements in New Oxford Street . . . . The shop was frequented by vagrants of every class, including foreigners, who, with moustache, well-brushed hat, and seedy clothes—consisting usually of a frock-coat buttoned to the chin, light trousers, and boots gaping at each lofty step—might be seen making their way to Buckeridge Street to regale upon cabbage, which had been boiled with a ferocious pig's head or a fine piece of salt beef. From 12 to 1 o'clock at midnight was chosen by these ragged but proud gentlemen from abroad as the proper time for a visit to Mrs Dowling's.

"Most of the houses in Buckeridge Street were lodging-houses for thieves, prostitutes, and cadgers. The charge was fourpence a night in the upper rooms, and threepence in the cellars, as the basements were termed. If the beds were occupied six nights by the same parties, and all dues paid, the seventh night (Sunday) was not charged for. The rooms were crowded, and paid well. I remember seeing fourteen women in beds in a cellar, each of whom paid 3d. a night, which, Sunday free, amounted to 21s. per week. The furniture in this den might have originally cost the proprietor £7 or £8. At the time I last visited it, it was not worth more than 30s.

"Both sides of Buckeridge Street abounded in courts, particularly the north side, and these, with the connected backyards and low walls in the rear of the street, afforded an easy escape to any thief when pursued by officers of justice. I remember on one occasion, in 1844, a notorious thief was wanted by a well-known criminal officer (Restieaux). He was known to associate with some cadgers who used a house in the rear of Paddy Corvan's, near Church Street, and was believed to be in the house when Restieaux and a serjeant entered it. They went into the kitchen where seven male and five female thieves were seated, along with several cadgers of the most cunning class. One of them made a signal, indicating that someone had escaped by the back of the premises, in which direction the officers proceeded. It was evident the thief had gone over a low wall into an adjoining yard. The pursuers climbed over, passed through the yards and back premises of eleven houses, and secured him in Jones Court. There were about twenty persons present at the time of the arrest, but they offered no resistance to the constables. It would have been a different matter had he been apprehended by strangers.

"In Bainbridge Street, one side of which was nearly occupied by the immense brewery of Mieux & Co., were found some of the most intricate and dangerous places in this low locality. The most notorious of these was Jones Court, inhabited by coiners, utterers of base coin, and thieves. In former years a bull terrier was kept here, which gave an alarm on the appearance of a stranger, when the coining was suspended till the course was clear. The dog was at last taken away by Duke and Clement, two police officers, and destroyed by an order from a magistrate.

"The houses in Jones Court wee connected by roof, yard, and cellar with those in Bainbridge and Buckeridge Streets, and with each other in such a manner that the apprehension of an inmate or refugee in one of them was almost a task of impossibility to a stranger, and difficult to those well acquainted with the interior of the dwellings. In one of the cellars was a large cesspool, covered in such a way that a stranger would likely step into it. In the same cellar was a hole about two feet square, leading to the next cellar, and thence by a similar hole into the cellar of a house in Scott's Court, Buckeridge Street. These afforded a ready means of escape to a thief, but effectually stopped the pursuer, who would be put to the risk of creeping on his hands and knees through a hole two feet square in a dark cellar in St. Giles' Rookery, entirely in the power of dangerous characters. Other houses were connected in a similar manner. There was a communication from one back window to another by means of large spike nails, one row to hold by, and another for the feet to rest on, which were not known to be used at the time we refer to.

"In Church Street were several houses let to men of an honest but poor class, who worked in omnibus and cab-yards, factories, and such other places as did not afford them the means of procuring more expensive lodgings. Their apartments were clean and their way of living frugal.

"Other houses of a less reputable character were very numerous. One stood on the corner of Church Street and Lawrence Street, occupied by the most infamous characters of the

district. On entering the house from Lawrence Lane, and proceeding upstairs, you would find on each floor several rooms connected by a kind of gallery, each room rented by prostitutes. These apartments were open to those girls who had fleeced any poor drunken man who had been induced to accompany them to this den of infamy. When they had plundered the poor dupe, he was ejected without ceremony by the others who resided in the room; often without a coat or hat, sometimes without his trousers, and occasionally left on the staircase naked as he was born. In this house the grossest scenes of profligacy were transacted. In pulling it down a hole was discovered in the wall opening into a timber-yard which fronted High Street—a convenient retreat for anyone pursued.

"Opposite to this was the Rose and Crown public house, resorted to by all classes of the light-fingered gentry, from the mobsman and his 'Amelia' to the lowest of the street thieves and his 'Poll'. I the tap-room might be seen Black Charlie the fiddler, with ten or a dozen lads and lasses enjoying the dance, and singing and smoking over potations of gin and water, more or less plentiful according to the proceeds of the previous night—all apparently free from care in their wild carousals. The cheek waxed pale when the policeman opened the door and glanced round the room, but when he departed the merriment would be resumed with vigour.

"The kitchens of some houses in Buckeridge Street afforded a specimen of life in London rarely seen elsewhere even in London, though some in Church Lane do so now on a smaller scale. The kitchen, a long apartment usually on the ground-floor, had a large coke fire, along with a sink, water-tap, one or two tables, several forms, a variety of saucepans, and other cooking utensils and was lighted with a gas jet. There in the evenings suppers were discussed by the cadgers an alderman might almost have envied—rich steaks and onions, mutton and pork chops, fried potatoes, sausages, cheese, celery, and other articles of fare, with abundance of porter, half-and-half and tobacco.

"In the morning they often sat down to a breakfast of tea, coffee, eggs, rashers of bacon, dried fish, fresh butter, and other good things which would be considered luxuries by working people, when each discussed his plans for the day's rambles, and arranged as to the exchange of garments, bandages, etc., considered necessary to prevent recognition in those neighbourhoods recently worked.

"Their dinners were taken in the course of their rounds, consisting generally of the best of the broken victuals given them by the compassionate, and wee eaten on one of the doorsteps of some respectable street, after which they would resort to some obscure public house or beer-shop in a back street or alley to partake of some liquor.

"Heaps of good food were brought home and thrown, on a side-table, or into a corner, as unfit to be eaten by those 'professional' cadgers—food which thousands of the working men of London would have been thankful for. It was given to the children who visited these lodging-houses. The finer viands, such as pieces of fancy bread, rolls, kidneys, mutton and lamb, the gentlemen of the establishment reserved for their own more fastidious palates.

"On Sunday many of the cadgers stayed at home till night. They spent the day at cards, shove-halfpenny, tossing, and other amusements. Sometimes five or six shillings were staked on the table among the party of about ten of them at cards, although coppers were the usual stakes . . . The life of a cadger is not in many instances a life of privation. I do not speak (says Mr. Hunt) of the really distressed, to whose wants too little attention is sometimes paid. I allude to beggars by profession, who prefer a life of mendicancy to any other. There are among them sailors, whose largest voyage has been to Tothill Fields prison, or to Gravesend on a pleasure trip. Cripples with their arms in slings, or feet, swathed in blood-stained rags, swollen to double size, who may be seen dancing when in their lodging at their evening revels. You may see poor Irish with from five to thirty sovereigns in a bag hung round their necks or in the waistband of their trousers; women who carry hired babies, or it may be a bundle of clothing resembling a child, on their back or breast, and other such-like imposters.

"Between Buckeridge Street and Church Lane stood Ivy Lane, leading from George Street to Carrier Street, communicating with the latter by a small gateway. Clark's Court was on its left, and Rat's Castle on its right. The castle was a large dirty building occupied by thieves and prostitutes, and boys who lives by plunder. On the removal of these buildings, in 1845, the massive foundations of an hospital were found, which had been built in the 12th Century by Matilda, Queen of Henry, daughter of Malcolm King of Scotland, for persons afflicted with leprosy.

"At this place criminals were allowed a bowl of ale on their way from Newgate to Tyburn.

"Maynard Street and Carrier Street were occupied by costermongers and a few thieves and cadgers. George Street, part of which still stands, consisted of lodging-houses for tramps, thieves, and beggars, together with a few brothels."

From George Street to High Street runs a Mews called Hampshire Hog Yard, where there is an old established lodging-house for single men, poor but honest.

The portion of the rookery now remaining, consisting of Church Lane, with its courts, a small part of Carrier Street, and a smaller portion of one side of Church Street, is now more densely crowded than when Buckeridge Street and its neighbourhood were in existence. The old Crown public house in Church Lane, formerly the resort of the most notorious cadgers, was in 1851 inhabited by Irish people, where often from twelve to thirty persons lodged in a room. At the back of this public house is a yard, on the right-hand side of which is an apartment then occupied by thirty-eight men, women, and children, all lying indiscriminately on the floor.

Speaking of other houses in this neighbourhood in 1851, Mr. Hunt states: "I have frequently seen as many as sixteen people in a room about twelve feet by ten, these numbers being exceeded in larger rooms. Many lay on loose straw littered on the floor, their heads to the wall and their feet to the centre, and decency was entirely unknown among them."

Now, however, the district is entirely changed, the inhabitants are rapidly rising in decency, cleanliness, and order, and the Rookery of St. Giles will soon be ranked among the memories of the past.

THE BAKER STREET BROADCAST

The only place for readers of the Moriarty paradigm and other steampunk'd Sherlockians to come together and share their thoughts, both de profundis and in extremis.

Email: letters@fringeworks.co.uk

www.facebook.com/moriartyparadigm

Welcome to the first iteration of the Baker Street Broadcast. Here, in an attempt to revive that most ancient tradition of written correspondence, we will be publishing letters and other communications (most probably gathered via teslagram), along with our considered responses, for the exclusive enjoyment of our readership.

Thanks for your teaser volume introducing the concept of a steampunk version of Sherlock Holmes. As a 180 year old I'm not sure whether I'll last long enough to see the series reach its conclusion, but I'm confident that my unborn great great grandson will. I intend to bombard you with the many Holmes tales I have recorded over the years in the hope that some of these stories will see print, and that they can be passed on down through the generations. You will forgive the one-sided nature of these stories, told as they are from my own perspective, but the relentless march of progress cannot afford to forget the contributions of those who once, in the face of the most overwhelming odds, changed the future. Indeed, now that my life is freed from the shackles of copyright protection, I shall take immense pleasure of seeing my stories last much longer than either Holmes or Doyle's Estates would want them to. Screw them. Screw them all.

- James R Moriarty

Well, James, many thanks for your letter and for the large tin trunk that accompanied it. I'm not quite sure how you managed to deliver the letter to us before our teaser volume was published, but we feel that as our oldest reader we would be doing you a disservice should we not reply. We will, of course, dip into your submissions, although they will require considerable editing as the use

of bitter expressions and foul language each time you put the name Sherlock Holmes to paper could otherwise prove to be distracting.

When I heard you were putting together a series of steampunk adventures starring Sherlock Holmes, I must confess I was a little dubious. We have already seen the great detective bastardised by the Asylum Films' T-Rex of the Baskervilles travesty (Sherlock Holmes, Asylum Films, 2010), and experienced the bike-riding Holmes and bionic-armed Watson of Steampunk Holmes by P C Martin, and when I first browsed a copy of Eliminating the Possible I was expecting more of the same. However, the attention to detail and the deference paid to Sherlock Holmes rather than to the steampunk genre impressed me— certainly enough to give your book a try. For a book of excerpts designed as a taster I found the book quite meaty, and got a real sense of the world, and the writing styles, you are trying to convey. I never thought I would say this of a steampunk book, but well done. The pay-off is anticipated with bated breath.

- Stuart Trueman

Expectations are a hard thing to meet blindly Stuart, and we hoped that by releasing a teaser volume in advance of complete stories that we would be better able to manage those expectations. These stories will be, first and foremost, traditional pulp and detective adventures, set against the backdrop of a carefully built world which, we hope, will present layers of interest to both the committed and the casual reader. The two steampunk versions of Holmes you mention follow the same tradition, but they simply have a different take on what does and doesn't make Sherlock Holmes. As you say, we put our portrayal of the great detective and his peers above the background and the sub genre.

As a steampunk I have been looking forward to some Sherlockian derring do for quite some time, and I felt it only fair to impart my expectations. I am particularly fond of cross-over fiction, particularly with Gothic horror and scientific romances. Shall we be seeing stories involving Dracula, Hyde, Moreau, Nemo, Robur and other larger than life geniuses?

- Basil Huntingdon-Whyte

Basil, sadly it is not our present intention to pursue cross-over nor supernatural adventures. We will explore these in other publications (Holmes vs. Zombies is already on our list), but it is our belief that they will be catered for by stand-alone stories. P C Martin's Steampunk Holmes involves

Captain Nemo, Guy Adams' 2013 novel *The Army of Dr Moreau* speaks for itself. Other past authors such as Fred Saberhagen (*Holmes vs. Dracula*) and Many Wade Wellman (*War of the Worlds*) have explored cross-overs quite successfully. We intend the science and fabric of the world we have created to obey its own internal logic. That said, we will be looking at some cross-over material, specifically relating to time travel and to works by Sir Arthur Conan Doyle (in particular the stories of Professor Challenger).

Ormond Sacker, Steampunk Detective has a nice ring to it. How will you be developing this idea? As a recurring character within your Holmes stories, as an alternate nemesis for Professor Moriarty, or as a stand-alone character in his own right?

- X Reed

As you probably know, X, Ormond Sacker was an early name considered by Doyle for the detective that became Holmes. He has been preserved in occasional fictions (e.g. as a coroner and associate of Professor Litefoot in Big Finish's audio series, *Jago and Litefoot*), but not in the form we are presenting. The answer to your question, we hope, will be all of the above, but in practical terms we need to see how the core series works first. If

there is interest (both from readers and writers) we may go on to commission a stand-alone novel or two, but our main reason for creating Sacker is to offer a viewpoint character for Holmes' earlier adventures, and in doing so to create a peer of comparable intellect rather than a more passive observer like Watson.

Oh great, just what we want. More Doyle plagiarism. More crappy Holmes pastiches. More steampunk books. More wasted shelf-space. Can't you be original instead? If you spent as much time focusing on decent mainstream fiction instead of on tired, recycled rubbish like this you might actually be worth reading.

- Anon.

Wow, Anon., thanks for the vote of support. It's a crowded market out there—100,000+ books are published in the UK every year—so there is room for all sorts. There's certainly enough choice out there for you to find and buy the kind of books you like without criticising others for having different tastes. Look at it this way, for over a century Holmes pastiche, fan fiction and parody has provided a gateway for new writers to enter the medium. Being able to emulate and replicate a style, form or genre is an important skill for a budding writer, and people have to cut their teeth somewhere. If you spent as much time practising your

writing skills across multiple genres and styles as you do moaning about something you're not even interested in, then I might not have had to edit and downsize your letter, nor would I have needed to correct your spelling to make you look sane when you put your point across.

I have been a Sherlock Holmes fangirl for years, and I just wanted to say that your new series is really raising the bar. I love the Sherlock TV series because it takes the spirit of Holmes and transplants it into another world, and that is the exact same feeling I got when I was reading Eliminating the Possible. I love steampunk, but what I love more is the idea that even familiar stories might gain a fresh spin, and that you will be developing a TV-style story arc that should keep us guessing. I've never paid much attention to small press stories, but I will now. It looks fantastic!! Sorry to gush, but The Moriarty Paradigm looks, to my mind, to be the most promising take on Holmes yet, and I can't wait to read the first proper mash-up.

- Kaitlyn

Ah, Kaitlyn, please gush away. By now you should have read The Scoundrel of Bohemia and, I hope, have stuck with us for this next instalment.

I actually picked up a copy of Eliminating the Possible because I heard about your article entitled 'What is Steampunk?' and I am now writing because I felt I need to respond.

First, steampunk is not what it was once—a literary experiment that tried and died. Modern steampunk has taken the name but not the baggage, and is a culture that is now inspiring fiction of a different kind. Your description of steampulp does fit that literary niche, but I take issue with the need to differentiate it from what has gone before. You speak of its origins like some kind of golden age, when in fact the golden age is now. Similarly, you are tying your concept down to the original adventures of Sherlock Holmes, which seems odd when we see how successfully the likes of Guy Ritchie and Steven Moffat/ Marl Gatiss have strayed from the original concept. Steampunk doesn't need to be historically accurate, nor does Sherlock Holmes need to be shackled by the works of Conan Doyle. What it needs is a healthy dose of engineering, romance, fantasy, strangeness and tea duelling.

- Air Captain Horace Jackstaff

Well Captain, we consider ourselves told! To be fair, steampunk is what you make of it—a happy camp of diverse chaps and chapesses who have a splendid time reading, costuming and being generally splendid. We will stick to our canons, and to our alternate history, but that doesn't mean we invalidate different approaches. The article in question should not be conflated with the series itself—it was a reflection on the history and evolution of steampunk, from where it was to where it is, with a literary focus because, well, we're all about the books. What really matters is that a good story is a good story, and that we are writing about an alternate world and an alternate Sherlock Holmes. Our rules are about him, not steampunk, and we have chosen to retain the elements we deem essential to his story.And to be fair, if you like modern steampunk, this issue does have faux zombies, battle armour, clockwork assassins and some genuinely toxic tea, so I'm hoping you'll take a sip and be duly refreshed. Be Splendid!

MORIARTY'S MISCHIEVOUS MISSIVE

Moriarty has secretly messaged minions. Holmes has already identified which squares contain the professor's message, but he needs your help to find and arrange the letters.

Across

1 Place frequented by Holmes on the Tottenham Court Road.

4 Burroughs' Lord as described in a famous American Holmes pastiche.

7 Moriarty falls into one of these at the end of a 1943 film.

9 A Cocaine solution.

11 Initials of the Overton rugby Captain.

12 Nicholas Meyer revealed that Moriarty was this during Holmes' childhood.

14 Watson's Regiment.

13 The original Baskerville home.

17 Holmes' original name, now that of a steampunk detective.

21 Unsystematic knowledge.

22 Charles Augustus _____, blackmailer.

23 221b appears above this.

25 Rat treks bee.

27 Moriarty's revealing vice.

28 Author of The Time Machine.

30 The Woman.

31 Doesn't know his gasogene from his bunsen burner.

32 Colour of the face at the window.

Down

1 Sherlock's scrapbooker.

2 They rebelled in 1857.

3 Bohemian capital.

5 One of the Four.

6 Ancestral French artist.

8 Moriarty's first name in William Gillette's Sherlock Holmes Stage Play.

10 Holmes never said this.

11 My father's brother only ate blue bread.

13 The Page.

15 Holmes said "There is nothing like first ____ evidence."

16 Gordon's steam boiler.

18 Latvian inventor of the Disintegration Machine.

19 Islands from whence Jonathan Small's accomplice came.

20 Original German name of the American Sherlock Holmes.

24 Location of Small's last stand.

25 The sibling age gap.

29 The Mackleton Priory.

CONTRIBUTORS

Darrel Bevan: Colour-blind, Darrel is a portrait and figure illustrator who, due to colour blindness, specialises in graphite illustration—mainly on black and white images. When he isn't producing photo-realistic pencil drawings, he teaches.

Sir Arthur Conan Doyle (1859 – 1930): Scotsman, doctor, sportsman, whale hunter, war correspondent and the world-renowned author responsible for the creation of Sherlock Holmes, Doyle was a social crusader who didn't shy from the realms of science fiction or, as it was known in his heyday, scientific romance. After starting his career with such tales, he became distracted by the adventures of Holmes, returning to the genre with the fantastic adventures of Professor Challenger. He never knew what steampunk was, but we are sure he wouldn't have given a damn.

Henry Mayhew (1812 – 1887): Journalist, playwright and one of the key social commentators of the nineteenth century, Mayhew co-founded and co-edited the legendary Punch magazine. His groundbreaking series of articles for the Morning Chronicle, later compiled as London Labour and the London Poor, drew attention to the underground cultures of London's poor, and remains as the most famous snapshot of the period, influencing the likes of Dickens, H. G. Wells and Conan Doyle himself.

Adrian Middleton: Writer, editor, publisher, local historian and the son of a real-life detective, Adrian is the creator of the Moriarty Paradigm, and willingly accepts the accusation that he is—for now—a Doyle plagiarist. When he isn't editing, he also writes original science fiction, fantasy an adventure stories.

ENDNOTE

Published in the July 1891 edition of the Strand Magazine, A Scandal in Bohemia was the third story to feature Sherlock Holmes, and the first of the fifty six short stories that established Holmes as the champion of the genre. When approaching the story with fresh eyes, and with a view to using the original text to create a steampunk mash-up, it became absolutely clear that any story based on an original text should share the credit with the original author. While Doyle never lived to see the dawn of steampunk, he did give his blessing to the rewriting of his early Sherlock Holmes play by William Gillette. It is therefore to Doyle and to Gillette that the greatest acknowledgement should be given—for without their collaboration, and the subsequent reinterpretations of Sherlock Holmes in the intervening years, the idea of steampunking the Holmes canon just wouldn't have felt right.

Of the many authors whose re-imaginings have helped to shape Holmes, Watson and Moriarty's future adventures, it is to those who may—if they were alive today—have joined in and written for a series such as the Moriarty paradigm, that we want to give special credit: John Kendrick Bangs, August Derleth, Philip Jose Farmer, Arnould Galopin, John Gardner, Edward D Hoch, Jean Ray, and Vincent Starrett.

FIND OUT MORE ABOUT FRINGEWORKS BY SCANNING THE QR CODE BELOW

www.fringeworks.co.uk

MORIARTY PARADIGM

ALSO AVAILABLE...

ELIMINATING THE POSSIBLE
ed. Adrian Middleton

Imagine the richly detailed Victorian London of Sherlock Holmes reinvented as a steampunk world created by the criminal genius of his arch-nemesis, Professor James Moriarty. Airships. Ray Guns. Moonshots. Tesla. Time Machines. Welcome to The Moriarty paradigm. Eliminating the Possible uses a remarkable series of excerpts, articles and original fiction to provide the introduction to an entirely new Holmes canon. Filled with all the familiar tropes of the steampunk genre, the Moriarty paradigm brings together a number of modern writers to reintroduce readers to the mystery and adventures of Sherlock Holmes.

THE LAVENDER MEN
by Adem Rolfe

When Watson is reunited with his loyal wartime orderly, he and Holmes become embroiled in the affairs of the New East India Company. Do dead soldiers fight for the crown? Only by investigating the dark secrets of Limehouse's Medical Ordnance Company can the great detective discover the truth.

A STUDY IN STEAMPUNK
by David A. McIntee

Returning to London to recuperate from injuries sustained over Afghanistan, Dr John Watson's quest for new accommodation brings him face to face with the eccentric Mr Sherlock Holmes, and his consulting rooms at 221B Baker Street. Plunged into the world of the scientific method of detection, the physician finds that he has not, after all, left death and mayhem in his past. He soon finds himself embroiled in a murder mystery involving coded messages, Her Majesty's Aeronautical Service, and the ever-present shadow of Professor James Moriarty. With no shortage of suspects, and the best brains of Scotland Yard left baffled, it is up to the self-styled Consulting Detective, and the recuperating Surgeon-Lieutenant, to learn to work together in unravelling the politics of the People of the Clouds, and to bring to an end an invisible killer's reign of terror.